Pseudo Stars

Anthony J. Langford

Pseudo Stars

For Nell and Tilly

Pseudo Stars
ISBN 978 1 76041 440 5
Copyright © Anthony J Langford 2017
www.anthonyjlangford.com
Front cover image: Jamie Noble Frier
Back cover image: Marjo Klingenberg

First published 2017 by
GINNINDERRA PRESS
PO Box 3461 Port Adelaide 5015
www.ginninderrapress.com.au

Contents

The Last Laugh

It's never how you imagine when you start out.

They sit next to each other by the table. She is slumped forward, her head resting on her forearm, asleep. She's eighty-four. Her dementia is in formidable flight. She doesn't talk much at all any more, a word out of context, scattered like autumn leaves. There are no reactions to gauge emotion. Most of the time she is quietly preoccupied with her doll. Plastic head, hands, feet. Cushy body. Therapy doll, they call it. It does something for her. Perhaps. It's hard to know what is left. What is observed. What is felt.

His left hand is on her back. His trolley walker by his right side. His mobility is worse than hers, yet he can still shuffle around. Only a matter of time, though. He's ninety-one and while hard of hearing, even with an aid, his eyesight is good, clarity of mind edgy. All things considered.

They married when he was twenty-six. The only time they were apart, aside from brief work trips, was when she was admitted to this place. Three long years ago. He followed…must be coming up twelve months? And while they don't live in the same unit (she's high-care), they are in the same facility.

He visits daily. An hour is enough. It used to be longer. Now there doesn't seem much point. A tad harsh but it depresses him. She never reacts at all. He used to talk to her, back when there was some response. Now he merely sits by her side, sometimes with his hand on her forearm. Other times simply maintaining a presence. An act of allegiance.

She doesn't always fall asleep. Though, now that he thinks about it, it's becoming more common. He wonders if soon that's all she'll ever do. Become bedridden, like those other unfortunate souls. How long? That's all that's left. Analyse the passing of the days. The minutes. One would expect more thoughts in the past, and there are those recalls of course. Yet the present is strong. Too hard to dismiss entirely. Especially with the bright lighting, the television drone and the incoherent cries of other residents. Then there's the smell. That original but distasteful mix of cleaning products, urine, mouldy clothes and mouldy bodies. He can't get used to it. This is not a place he can get used to. He does try. It would make life – for want of a better term, more palatable. Yet he's too old for artifice.

He's been through worse. Well, it felt worse at the time. The death of his parents. Hers too. His brother's accident. That's what they called those sort of events in those days. There was the miscarriage of course. Then success. He was elated. They both were. Though memory of those first few years is scant. He was always working. Three hundred employees beneath him. Manufacturing deadlines to maintain. There was a lot of hardship. A lot of yelling. It was all-consuming. It seemed so important. He allowed it to overtake his life. He welcomed it. Endless meetings, hotel rooms, shifting people around, analysing graphs, statistics. There was Saturday golf and Sunday lunches, but really, he missed most of his daughter's childhood. Men didn't have an active role in parenthood like they do now. It was a woman's domain. It was his role to provide for them. The wheels of progress (and profit) slow for no man. He was an exceptional provider. However, if he's honest, he wasn't much of a father. He came to be aware of it in time but it was too late. A cordial relationship. None of those unbreakable blood bonds. That's just not him. No wonder his daughter cast them both into the home. Not long after he signed everything over to her. Kapow. Right between the shoulder blades. Sixty years of venom dispensed in one strike. He's partly to blame but the spoilt brat was given practically…

'Cup of tea, Mr Twohey?'

'Huh?'

'Cup of tea? Piece of cake?'

Trolley time.

'No, thank you.'

'Are you sure? Coffee? Water?'

'Nothing.'

'How about Mrs Twohey? Should I leave something?'

What do you think, you silly cow? 'Nothing.'

'Okay. If you need anything, just ask.'

He sighs. He doesn't have time for these people. He doesn't have time for anyone. There's some irony. He has every minute of the day at his disposal. Still. Social etiquette isn't easy at his age. He's civil enough. Just enough. There are no goals to reach. No agendas at play. No one to impress. Not even his wife. She was mightily impressed many times. He relished each and every one. Even now he's still hoping she'll look up and say, 'You're wonderful, my darling. You do such a fine job of looking after me.'

If only. Her eyes are closed. Mouth half open. No drool. She looks almost normal. As though she could indeed wake up at any moment and say, 'My God, Jonathan. What is this horrid place? Take me home immediately.'

And he'd laugh and off they'd go, hand in hand, just like…

He sighs. More deeply this time. That thought plunged his mood, enough to make his muscles sag. He rubs her back. No response. He sighs again. Time to leave. No point trying to wake her. The medication puts her under quite thoroughly. She won't know who he is anyway.

He manoeuvres his trolley closer. He places his hands on each grip. He bears down with his arms and feet into the floor. He begins to rise but his weak knees only allow him to make it halfway. He farts and slumps back to the chair. He grunts, then sniggers. He looks over to the care assistant with the trolley. She's helping a woman drink tea from one of those plastic cups. She must have heard him but didn't flinch. She's used to it of course. And worse. He isn't. He's a man of sophistication. He still maintains his dignity, despite his body trying to usurp him. It was certainly loud. He chuckles again, unable to help himself. He looks to his wife. Inert. She'd be horrified. She was always a stickler for decorum. That sort of thing was never tolerated in her home.

'I just farted,' he says to her and breaks into a guffaw which takes fire like an unyielding kookaburra. 'I farted. Ha ha ha ha ha ha ha ha ha ha ha ha.'

The Loop

He steps casually into the train carriage. He's only a few stops from the city loop so takes up position near the doors. Across from him sits a dishevelled young woman, casually eating a cheeseburger. Her toddler, a boy about two, stands in front of her with fries scrunched in both sweaty hands. Aside from his nappy, he's naked. It may be summer but surely it's not hot enough to justify his lack of clothing or bare feet upon the grimy floor. The young man frowns. He quickly determines that it's nothing to do with him. He gazes at his phone, hoping his friend had not notified of a late change to their rendezvous, as he had been known to.

'Eat ya fries,' says the mother, who doesn't look particularly healthy, due to lack of sleep, or a bad diet, which seems likely, or perhaps it's something more, like drugs.

The young man could not discern, though surmised that it could be a combination of all those things.

'No, no, no,' the boy says, swaying side to side against the movement of the train, beginning to shake his head and threatening to topple in protest.

'Don't be a brat or you'll get it,' she spits.

'No!' the boy shouts.

In a surprisingly swift manoeuvre, his mother tosses her food to one side, grips the toddler by the upper arm and smacks him hard on the bottom. The boy does not cry, as this is nothing new, though throws the fistful of fries towards the doors.

'You little shit!' She whacks him again, and again, his swollen diaper protecting him from the full force yet he tries to twist himself from her grasp, without success.

'Don't do that!' the young man says instinctively.

'You don't get it,' she says, though she ceases hitting. 'He's a nightmare!'

The young man rubs his chin, not knowing what to say. A middle-aged woman, who's approaching the doors in preparation for the next stop, says, 'The poor child should have some clothes on. The floor's filthy.'

'What would you know? Mind ya own business, bitch!' She scoops up her child, who merely squirms and begins to shriek like a tortured mouse. His mother slaps his pudgy right leg with a high-pitched crack in an attempt to subdue him. It doesn't work. She does it again.

As the train draws to a halt, the older woman mutters, 'That's shocking.'

'Piss off, ya pill-poppin' whore!'

The young man stands, wanting to rescue the child but having witnessed enough, steps over the boy's fries and disembarks with the middle-aged woman.

'That's just terrible,' she says.

Though lacking words only moments before, the young man is promptly filled with indignation. 'What sort of mother is that? We should report her. Maybe the police can arrest her.'

'There's no point. The child's not even crying. I imagine he's used to it, poor thing.'

As the doors close and the train begins to move, the mother stands, her toddler still squirming fruitlessly under her right arm. She awards the onlookers with the classic one-fingered salute.

Fabulous Flaw-finding Phil

He strolls purposefully through the chaotic food court. He had promised himself to nurture calmness. But a hunter in the jungle is incapable of navel-gazing.

A Muslim woman stuffs her lunch rubbish into the bright yellow bin.

'That's for recycling,' he says. He points to the red bin. 'Try that one next time.'

She does not look at him, or even acknowledge him, but she does hesitate.

He moves to an outdoor area, chicken schnitzel focaccia in hand. To the left sit two policemen having lunch. Opposite them sits an attractive but a somewhat class-starved young woman, busy talking at them, it seems, and not to them. He chooses the table closest to them, curiosity having stung him, sun streaming from its one thirty-four p.m. position.

Pide virtually untouched in front, she peals sentence-less about her rude colleague and how he never says hello. The men watch and listen. Seemingly. Or perhaps they're simply watching those light-refracting pushed-up bosoms. It's hard to be certain.

Phil tackles his focaccia, trying to unravel more, but finds her soliloquy tiresome. He soon tunes out. He observes the traffic. The law-breaking fools distract him, as is often the case. The system would work perfectly, if people managed to follow the basic procedures. Awareness. Speed limit. Indicate and so on. It's that ten per cent that tarnishes the game board. Maybe twenty.

She's finally stopped talking. It's her colleague's turn. The one with the beard. Within seconds, she's turned her attention to her phone.

Scanning and replying. It seems that only the other policeman is taking stock.

Our man Phil studies her. It's not a message check. She's thumb browsing. Almost a minute passes before Phil makes his play. He redirects his chair to face them. Her tits are nice. Pity.

'I've got to say, I love the irony.'

The two men turn to him. The woman shifts her eyes but not her head.

'You were just complaining that your rude colleague doesn't say hi to you and yet these gentlemen just listened to your story and as soon as it's their turn you're straight to your phone. That's the definition of irony. Perfectly displayed. Textbook really.'

'Do you know him?' asks beardless cop.

'Noooooo!' she cries with an upward inflection like a grossed-out child.

'All right, mate. Take off.'

'Forgive the pun there. Facebook. Textbook. Texting. Delicious.'

'What is your problem?' she says. 'You're so full of shit!'

'I could possibly be, after this focaccia.'

Beardless cop stands. 'Let's see your driver's licence, please.'

'I don't drive, officer.' Phil doesn't take his eyes off her. 'Too many idiots on their phones.'

'What a rude prick,' she says.

'More irony. Thank you.'

Phil is made to show his identification, including his driver's licence. 'My focaccia is getting cold.'

'Shoulda kept your mouth shut then, huh,' she says, phone still in her palm.

'Focaccia you.'

'Watch it, mate.'

'I didn't swear, officer. I don't believe I've crossed any legal line.'

Regardless, Phil receives a customary grilling. He takes it on the chin. Give them what they want and it will pass, which it does soon enough, his objective already reached. While being questioned, she's back to her phone. What a waste of effort. The lesson is already lost.

Thursday and Friday are his days off. It's a mixed blessing. He enjoys not working when everyone else does, but he also encounters the rush rush, which eventually brings out the mindless moron in seemingly rational people. The thing is, the dual cop integration is now on repeat. It's how his head works. The way they conducted themselves was so accusatory. So patronising.

On the way home, he encounters a council worker noisily blowing leaves with his phallic symbolised machine.

'Hey, mate!' Phil signals. The man switches the machine off. 'You realise that you're just moving those leaves around, right? Any wind that comes along and it's back to where they started again.'

'Humph.' The noise returns.

Phil shouts, 'Get a broom and save us all a headache!' He moves on, mumbling, 'Street sweeping was a trade. Now those sweeper trucks blow their shit over everyone's cars. Fuck it. Let's just 3-D print a skyscraper and be done with tradies altogether.'

The next situation occurred the following morning, a Friday. Phil's Sunday. A rare but enthusiastic morning stroll around the park pumps the blood. It gives rise to a range of thoughts, ideas, plans, one of which is chemically based and there's no eliminating that once it surfaces. Not fully. It's like a reality TV, selfie, vlogger version of the Loch Ness Monster. Nowhere to hide, especially as, in modern terms, it seeks the opposite. The monster is up for air and is gasping. You could be assuming one of two scenarios here; so let's see which one it becomes.

He enters his apartment building and pushes the button on the only lift, ardently seeking his slice of sanctuary on level four. The lift makes its way from level seven but it soon stops at three. It's eight thirty-ish, no doubt workers en route to the grind.

It lingers. And remains stationary. Longer than he's ever witnessed. Patience is a virtue, they say, but right now his dump truck is reaching full capacity and it's ready for the tray to tip. He's busting for privacy.

Someone's got to be holding the door open. Waiting for another? A family member? Some cunt. This is ridiculous.

If he yells at the doors, they could probably hear him up the shaft. For God's sake. It's like he's back in primary school with the time between needing to go and having to go being mere seconds. It was that bloody homemade fruit smoothie. Never again!

With each passing second, there's the expectation that the lift will start to descend, hence his hesitation to yell out. Surely any second now. Another resident behind him. An older Asian woman. Holding her up too. How selfish.

The number abruptly changes to two. 'About time.' Number two. He appreciates the irony but not as much as he normally would. This is urgent now. How dare they?

One. Oh yes. He's going to let them have it. He manoeuvres to block the doors as they slide open. Inside is a man. Thirties. Australian? Also a woman. Asian. Chinese. Younger. Ah that's it. He was waiting for the girlfriend.

Phil blocks the doors. 'I thought the lift was broken. Thank God you're okay!'

'Uh, yep.'

Phil does not shift. 'Are you sure you're okay? Should I call the paramedics to give you an oxygen check? I mean, you could have had a claustrophobic fit with all that time in there.'

'No, no. Excuse me...' says the suited Caucasian.

'Anxiety is a strange beast. Panic attacks.'

'Yeah, I'm late for work so can you move out...'

'No wonder you're late. So much time in the lift.' He's tormenting himself more than them but there's a point to be made and they're damn well going to get it.

'I said excuse me.'

'I'm late too – for a dump. But you don't seem to give a shit about that!' Pun intended.

'What the hell?'

The girlfriend steps forward. 'Move.' She pushes past. Her older partner quickly takes up her slipstream.

'As long as you're okay!' echoes Phil. 'The two of you star spinning wonders!'

He enters the lift, the befuddled elderly Chinese woman reluctantly following him.

'Do you know those two?' he asks.

She does not look at him.

'A gift to mankind, they are. Centre of the Universe!'

Despite his flippancy, Phil realises he's in serious trouble. He shuffles to the rear of the lift and forces his butt cheeks against the wall. The woman presses three.

'Ah, number four, if you please.'

She ignores him.

'Four! Push four, for fuck's sake.' Alas, he cannot move to do it himself. It seems she is ignoring him deliberately for who knows what reason. 'Four. Please. Pleee…'

The lift stops and she exits without a glance.

The immediate threat eliminates his anger. He's screwed. He has to move forward in order to hit the button of choice. Only one floor. Goddamn it. He takes half a step forward. The slimy slithering snake is snoopy and more soupy than seasoned. Oh shit! Bum back to the wall. It's bad. He's forced to slide against the wall, awkwardly into the corner and on towards the control panel. How will he make it from the lift door to his? Cross that bridge…

Sliding. Reaching. Here he goes. CLUNK! Lift is descending.

'Fuuuucckkkkk!'

All hope lost, Phil, or more precisely, his treacherous arsehole betrays him with all its power and horror.

'Ooohh, my God.'

Thirty-three minutes later, Phil redresses after his shower, his trashed jeans in the laundry sink and more than likely heading for the bin. The world is filled with idiocy and self-absorption. Whoever termed 'Fool's Paradise' had more wisdom than Socrates. No wonder the poor bastard killed himself. Talk about self-sacrifice in order to make a statement. Phil had followed in the great Greek's footsteps. It wasn't worth it. Was it? Then he smiles. And suddenly he's laughing his arse off. Literally.

In aged care, there's an anomaly called 'sundowning'. Many dementia patients come alive in the mid-afternoon. By four thirty-four, the moment Phil left his building, he was well and truly 'worked up'.

Admittedly it was a chaotic intersection at the best of times. Recent events, aside from the explosion of 'self', had him on edge. Not so much the cop mini-interrogation or the lift shit. He could deal with that just fine as it was a justifiable stance and who doesn't feel satisfied with treading the path of the righteous? Shame can last forever but only one had been witness to his shit storm, the dishevelled Sri Lankan chap from level two and he wasn't exactly an aromatic representative from Chanel No. 5.

No. What had really bothered him that afternoon was the Lebanese woman he had passed on the way back down the street. He'd been hoping to see her around again as she had said that she was a local but it had been weeks (six, seven?) since their first and only meeting. It had been a chance encounter at the local park. The ten-minute conversation which followed felt like thirty minutes or even longer. In fact, he had thought of little else for days after.

So when he saw her that very day, he lit up like a blood transfusion. And you know what? Despite her apparent recognition – oh, she had recognised him all right – she merely half-smirked…more of a sneer, a cringe. Yet not a word. Not a single word. What was her game? What had he done wrong? Nothing. It was nasty. Cruel. It made no sense. Had he said something at the end of that conversation to cause this turnabout? Their interaction was brief but the replays and imagining scenarios in the weeks that followed was a relationship in bloom. For Phil.

He entered the pedestrian crossing. His defences were already to the fore due to the female driver of the car, and her companion, sitting three-quarters over the pedestrian line. A good fifty-plus people must step around them and potentially into traffic. Why were they so calm about it? The car behind her had realised her error and allowed a gap for her to correct it. The offer not taken for her to reverse, too busy chatting to her young passenger.

The injustice could not be allowed to pass unaddressed. As he slowly passed the cars, his eyes drilled into her, until she noticed him. He raised his right hand in reference to her questioning, seemingly lost on her. She turned her lips up in disgust.

He stops. 'Why don't you back up?'

She waves her hand in defiance. Who is this shit pickle?

He reads her indignation. Her instinctive hatred. Her rejection. 'Why don't you back up? So selfish!'

Her chin protrudes. Knuckles seize. Her domineering brother rises in her mind's eye. Her spiteful teacher returns. She doesn't have to put up with this shit. She's an adult now. She's in charge. Plus her friend next to her is a conduit to the wider network. They will all know. Her spine electrifies. That Aussie fuck! She pumps the accelerator, ever so briefly, just to scare the dick. Something jars, foot on brake, a scream, people staring now, something in front, more screams, pointing at her, yelling. Did she? Now she engages reverse. The car behind. A metre or two. A bump. More screams. Oh God, she's hit something. Run over. Backwards. And forwards too?

Screams. Shouting. Anarchy erupts. Phil treads casually away. Not his pantomime to own. People need to take responsibility. He's been proven right. The crazies are in charge of the funny farm but it's the sane ones who handed over control. A single fool can ruin a hundred. The proof is in his pudding. He's the modern-day superhero. Undercover. Unnoticed. Unappreciated. Unloved. The price of truth is never more costly than to the whistle-blower.

Let no good deed go unpunished.

The world will benefit, ultimately, yet some poor fucker has to get their hands dirty. And Phil's are filthy. Ah, such is life.

Ding Ding – Man of the Fringe

Ding Ding. Most of the townsfolk knew him by name and by reputation. He was a bum and mad with drink. He had been a boxer. So they said. I never knew whether that was actually true yet it appeared genuine. People drove by or yelled from across the street, 'Ding Ding!' He would shape up and begin whacking the air. They thought it was hilarious. He was far from the only drunk in town but he was the most memorable. To me, it seemed he had always been there.

I was seventeen. My grandfather would drop me off in the centre of town on his way to work. I would have to wait about an hour for the bus that would take me to a farm. I was a member of a group of young people building a mud-brick house, part of an unemployment scheme. It was winter and freezing. All that water and mud. I hated it but was told to keep busy. I had no ability in the art of manual labour. I don't think it did anything for me at all other than perhaps erode my confidence, the little that was there. Yet it's how I met Ding Ding.

While waiting for that morning bus, I would sit in the baby change room in a toilet block. It was the only place to keep out of the chill. I never saw a parent there, certainly not at that time of day, and I would read. Others began showing up, the local drunks, waiting for the nearby booze shop to open.

I was shy and continued reading but soon enough, I got to know them. A middle-aged Aussie guy called Dave was the talkative one. He was lucid, articulate and, maybe due to the time of day, sober. He seemed like an everyday Joe. His ball belly and bulbous crimson nose gave him away. There were others who came and went. Guys not so friendly. Yet Ding Ding was Dave's constant companion and his polar opposite. He was Aboriginal and quite short. He was also the silent type. In fact, he never spoke. Not a single word. I knew of his notoriety and was a little intimidated.

After subsequent mornings, he began to warm to me. He would nod his head my way and occasionally shake my hand. He'd listen to Dave's stories like I did and there were plenty. Many of them, it seemed to my young ears, were embellished. Yet we were grateful, as though the stories stole the chill from the air.

Dave had it all at one stage. A wife, kids and a property in Tasmania. Undisclosed personal and financial matters got the better of him. He sought refuge in the bottle, which was no good refuge at all. He freely admitted that the booze dictated his life. Don't ever drink, he told me. The warning was already too late, but I appreciated it, especially in hindsight. The drink got its claws into me later on but never to the extent of those poor souls. At least, not yet. Alcoholism. The disease of 'yets'.

Dave told me that Ding Ding had esteem around town for challenging anyone who imitated the boxing bell. I nodded, pretending not to know. The man himself smiled. As Ding Ding was always present, I was never able to ask Dave more about him or why he did not talk.

Dave and whoever else was around, which wasn't many in those early hours, talked about politics and current affairs. How they kept up with all of these events, I wasn't quite sure. Being young, I didn't think it possible that they could inhabit a normal home life and that, somehow, they lived in a parallel universe. This, of course, many years before the personal phone and internet. The change room, our shared space, was the one and only portal.

Sometimes in the afternoon, on the way from the farm back to town, the bus would drive past the town's main park. I would spy a large group of drinkers gathered there, Dave and Ding Ding amongst them. They were well into their day's activities. I assumed they lived on the streets but, to be honest, I don't know where they spent their nights.

I told them how I had to work for any unemployment benefits, a new scheme then, but found it so exhausting that there was no time for any job hunting. The irony not lost on my inexperienced self. Irrespective of the details, Dave was sympathetic. And that was enough.

I told them how I was living with my grandparents. My parents were working-class and building a house and doing all of the work themselves. They were forced to live in a tiny caravan on site. There wasn't enough room for my two younger siblings and me as well. I hadn't been getting on with my parents, so I think the arrangement was convenient. The men listened. It prompted them to open up about their own childhoods. Difficult. Rural. Sometimes abusive. Maybe my situation wasn't so bad after all.

They talked about women and other things that I wasn't privy to or didn't understand at the time. Sometimes I sat and read my book and we merely shared the space, with a mutual acceptance and perhaps an unspoken understanding that we were deemed to be on the outskirts of the ordered ways of the world.

Almost four months later, I landed a job as an apprentice in a printing firm. The morning conversations with those men of the streets came to an end. Occasionally, I would see Ding Ding around town, looking dishevelled and alcohol encumbered yet without his faithful counterpart. He looked worse for wear each time. After a while, I didn't see him at all. I don't know what happened to him, or Dave and the others. Perhaps they moved out of town. More than likely they passed away somewhere, perhaps in one of those parks or back streets. I can only guess. Yet I will never forget those mornings, the odd but respectful gatherings of those on the fringe.

Would You Like an Experience With That?

Placing order

Only three roads into their tiny town. They are all quiet but this one is literally dead. It's Thursday. School holidays. 1.11 p.m.

'Here he comes,' Mark says, straddling his bike.

'Cool,' says Brittany, similarly positioned.

'Fucking Coke and Chips.'

A man ambles towards them by the road's edge. His head is down. Greasy, unkempt orange hair.

'He doesn't know we're here,' she says.

'Dumb arse.'

The thirteen-year-olds had made an assumption. While never one to eyeball others, Coke and Chips is well aware of what lies in front of him. He's a thirty-four-year-old man. However, he cannot avoid them. There is only one path from his home that he shares with his elderly mother. His trajectory does not alter. His directness could be misconstrued for assertiveness but his routine is so ingrained that there is little thought to his methodology, thirty-four or no.

'Off to get ya coke and chips?' Mark spits as the man nears.

His demeanour and pace, albeit a slow one, do not diminish.

Brittany adds her part to the one-way exchange. 'That stuff will make you fat, you know.'

'Ha.' Mark scoffs. 'Too late.'

'Ha ha ha.'

It's true. Coke and Chips has a bowling ball stomach and an unattractive bulge just above his groin. Aside from that, the rest of him appears quite slim.

He continues as always, peering at the ground as though monitoring the progress of his feet. As though he had all the time in the world. Given his simple daily routine, perhaps he does.

'Hey, mate,' Mark says, still with his bike in hand, 'Why do you always eat coke and chips? Don't you get sick of that shit?'

He remains mute. The proximity between them is within the context of awkwardness yet the man maintains his trajectory.

Mark stares as if to challenge but it's not returned.

The man shuffles past, the barest hint of his bottom showing above his pants.

'Did you see that?' Mark asks.

'What?'

'The way he walked past like that. What an arsehole.'

'You could almost see his arsehole.' Brittany begins to laugh. She finds herself unable to stop.

Mark fails to see anything funny. 'He didn't even move.'

Brittany does not grasp Mark's affronted pride, which is strong at the best of times, but twofold in the presence of his long-standing friend.

'I'm gunna cut up that guy's face.'

'Don't be stupid.' She concentrates a second. 'With what?'

Mark stares after the shambling pathetic figure. He is overcome with hatred, whereas before, the man had been a source of fun. Mark had been out to impress Brittany. This isn't cool. 'Coke and Chips fuck!'

'What a loser.' Brittany looks about. What should they do now? Holidays can be a pretty lame time in their little town. 'Let's go.'

'I'm gunna get him on the way back.'

'Huh?'

'I'm gunna fuck that guy up.'

'How?'

'You watch.'

'Aw, who cares about fat Chips and Coke?'

'Coke and fuckin' Chips.' Mark lets his bike fall. 'He'll be back soon. I'll be waiting.'

'Are you a super hero now? Ha ha.'

'You watch. I'll fuck him up.'

'Have you really got a knife?'

Mark moves a few feet, bends down and plucks a small rock from the ground. 'Help me find some more. Big ones.'

'He'll know it's you.'

'I don't care. I'm gunna smash his fat guts.'

'Ha ha. You're crazy.'

Waiting

They know he'll return soon. The man is as much a part of the town as the hairdresser or the monument in the park or the shaved grasses around the local church. Mark attempts to ride his bike with the front wheel fixed in the air. He can manage it for a few seconds only.

Brittany is interested for a bit, though not as mesmerised as he would like her to be. In actuality she is listless. 'Why don't we go to the river?' she suggests.

'Piss off.'

'This is boring.'

'Don't you wanna see me smash Coke and Chips?'

'Well…yeah. But what you gunna do? He's bigger than you.'

Mark pushes his bike into the grass. 'I'm gunna rock him, dickhead. What do you think I got the rocks for?'

She sighs.

He paces to the small pile of rocks that they had collected. 'I'll bring him down with just one. You watch.'

'I don't wanna get in trouble. Can't we go somewhere? I'm hungry. I might get chips too.'

'You wanna hang out with fat guts, do ya?'

There is only one place for such food. It has long-standing oil spray on the walls near the open grill. It's been running for forty years and the locals support it. It's not like there's competition. Some customers, especially one, are more reliable than the store clock. 1.20 p.m. Every. Single. Day.

'He's gross,' Brittany says.

'So watch me do it, okay?'

'Okay. But don't go too far. He's crazy, you know.'

As he moves to his bike, Brittany makes Mark aware of the shuffling figure returning.

Mark hurries to his rock pile, scooping up one approximately the length of his thumb. Not a huge rock but a good size for throwing.

Brittany steps off the track and folds her arms. She realises that she's not excited like Mark. She even has a tinge of butterflies. She doesn't want to be here any more.

Order complete

Mark is on the track, right hand feeling the weight of the rock. 'Coke and Chips! Makes you fat! Fat fuck!'

The man advances without hesitation.

'Fatty fat, fat guts! Eat too much Coke and chips!'

'You can't eat Coke, dumb ass.'

'Shut up!'

'Don't tell me to shut up!'

Despite the slow gait, Coke and Chips is on them before Mark has truly prepared himself. She has distracted him. He cannot aim the way he'd like. The dead eyes. The mask face. The ginger hair. The man boobs. Mark moves to one side and once again, the man breezes past, close enough to touch, yet never misses a beat. They can detect his freckles and the white puffy flesh above the belt line, like an eel wrapped around his waist.

'Coke and Chips. Gross.' Mark says, more like a quiet statement.

Brittany watches the man, somewhat relieved.

Mark looks to Brittany. Is she disappointed? She probably thinks he's a pussy. 'Yeah!' He turns, takes a short run up and hurls the rock.

It whizzes past the man's right shoulder. It's a good throw. Mark is reasonably agile, like many a young teenager.

Coke and Chips turns slightly, as if to follow the path the rock had taken. He slows. Briefly. Then moves on.

Mark runs a few more steps and with a burst of confidence propels a second rock at his target. A perfect pitch. It smashes just below the centre of the man's skull, and his neck seems to bounce forwards and back again. He does not fall or stumble, merely takes one more step and stops.

Brittany's mouth is wide open.

Coke and Chips touches the back of his head and looks at his hand. Is there red amongst the orange? Brittany can't tell.

Mark doesn't know whether to run…no, he can't. Not in front of Brittany. Should he throw another rock?

The man turns slowly on his heels like a smooth spit roast. In one hand he holds the bag containing his large box of chips and the Coke can. In the other, with palm upraised, fingers of glistening red. Yes. He is injured. He begins towards them.

Mark immediately backs up. His heart thumps like a rabbit ready to spring. He holds another rock at the ready.

Brittany remains transfixed, the man's eyes peering into hers. He is looking at her, isn't he? Walking. Towards. To do what? His face seems familiar. Eyes. Eyes of a person. He'd only been a distant figure, shuffling to and fro. Not even a real person. Coke and Chips. Like a robot. A fat pathetic…eyes. To her. Upon her. He stops, just outside her personal space barrier. He raises his arm, his plastic lunch bag dangling from it, slowly swinging. He offers it to her.

The natural thing to do is to take it. Which she does.

He does not look away from her. Is he going to say something? What's he thinking? He slowly turns and walks away. She can immediately see how wet his hair is. And the broken trail of blood down his back. Yet he does not appear to be affected by it. He shuffles on as always, empty-handed.

She turns to Mark. She has never seen such an expression. She can't decipher it, other than he looks weird. Maybe confused. But very still. Holding the rock. She looks back. Coke and Chips shuffles on. She half expects him to collapse. He doesn't. Soon, he is gone.

Digestion

Brittany spends a lot of time thinking about that moment. That event. A daytime hallucination which she did not realise she was in at the time. She has dreams about it. Nightmares. Too crazy to think about. He must love that food so much to have it every day. So why did he give it to her? Did he know that she wanted chips too? Did he read her mind?

She can't speak to Mark about it. Not in detail. She had called him a dickhead, but her emotions were too complex to unravel. How is she supposed to feel? What should she do? All she knows is that she is too embarrassed to tell her mother. Too horrified. Yes, that's the word. Horrified.

In a week, she stops hanging out with Mark. A week later, she refuses to acknowledge his existence at all.

Brittany ensures that she is never in town between one and two on any day, no matter what, for the rest of the year. And the next. And one day, the mysterious man was gone.

She never found out what happened to Coke and Chips. The store remains open but without any information as to its once infamous regular. Some folks say that he simply vanished.

By the time she is old enough to personally investigate such matters, Brittany is in the city and living with her boyfriend. She's contemplating a trip to Mexico or possibly even further south. Wouldn't it be interesting to see how different people lived?

Cock. Old?

There are some places in the world that are best left alone.

Life is painful, despite all our plans. It's a chaotic world, an indifferent Universe. Things only go wrong because we're so busy trying to make it right. In our heads, our future life is perfect. Our scenarios are flawless because we haven't factored in all the little details. We assume that they'll be all right (on the night). This story revolves around a middle-aged couple who wanted to live out a fantasy, that of the sexual variety.

'I don't know if it's such a good idea, Leopold,' she had said, even though he had told her repeatedly, 'I get turned on by the thought of watching you being fucked, Cecilia, and not being able to do anything about it. I want you to tie me to that chair and pretend I'm not there.'

The chair in question was by the end of the bed near the door. He had looked at it many times, his thoughts raging with diverse home theatre screenings.

The debate had raged on and off with all the pros and cons explored. No matter how many hours they had spent discussing it, the core scenario itself never folded up and vanished. Leopold held onto his fantasy, nursing it like a puppy.

Gradually, over time, she came around to the notion. Secretly she had begun to relish part of it, that of another man's hands on her body, lusting after her the way her husband could no longer do. In order to disguise her willingness, she had to raise a protracted resistance. Perhaps she took it too far. It went on for a year longer than it should have.

He was patient, yet determined to have his way.

The real issue for her was that she wasn't thrilled with the idea of her husband being in the room. In a very roundabout way, she had suggested to him that he might be better off being outside the boudoir while the deed took place or, better still, outside the house altogether. Wasn't it the torment that stimulated him and not the visualisation of the act? He insisted that you can't have a cat and mouse game without the mouse. Save for saying no, she had no other option but to agree. She hoped in time that he might be willing to modify the scenario and allow her more independence. In time, who knew, she might even request a stranger who was well endowed. Leopold wasn't what you would call big, but he was far too insecure to warrant bringing it up. Pun intended.

They joined an adult website with an expectant glee. They perused other couples and singles in their thirties, forties and fifties. It was a smorgasbord of flesh and fantasy. There were many others like themselves and some whose whims far exceeded their own. Cecilia was barely able to contain her joy at eyeing at least three great specimens of manhood. Each time she saw one, she tried to remember the man's profile handle, such as HotBod and BiggusDickus. She couldn't resist a snap glimpse at Leopold to see if he was sneakily studying her, lest he spy her silent girlish enthusiasm.

Several months went by. They chatted to many people and went as far as meeting one man, but it never went further than the local pub. In fact, it was Leopold who discovered that his feet were cold. Blue, bloodless and frozen.

'Why didn't you like him?' she asked.

'Dunno. Something was off. It just…didn't feel right.'

She sighed. She knew that she had to shift tack. The next time they arranged to meet a fellow at the same bar, she said, 'I don't want to keep playing this game.'

'Let's just see what he's like first.'

'Leopold, it's never going to be perfect. Maybe we should put it down as a fantasy and leave it there.'

'Let's see what he's like. He checked out pretty well.'

Leopold had inadvertently called Cecilia's bluff. She had subtly manipulated her husband into choosing laidbackguy4 as the next proposition. He was well hung, though not as monstrous as some of the profiles she had covertly masturbated to, but nevertheless, proportionately divergent to what she was accustomed.

When the pair reached the pub, it took them a little time to pick him out. He wasn't quite the picture of excellence he had displayed on his profile, though they had to concede neither were they. He was in his early thirties and in good shape. The fact that he was younger made them feel slightly intellectually superior, though Leopold felt somewhat old with his mild gut from beer and greying hair which was more salt than pepper.

They had a few drinks and returned home, two now three. The man sat stiffly on the couch, no longer in a neutral environment and subsequently less sure of himself, despite his admirable performance at the bar.

Leopold cracked a bottle of red, a decent drop, wanting to impress. The label was lost on the stranger, not being a wine connoisseur.

Cecilia sat on Leopold's favourite chair, making small talk, trying not to look down but hoping that the man's package was as attractive as its screen shot.

Leopold ensured that he was a visible presence in the room, as he yanked the cork from the bottle, feeling in charge, as though he was the parent and the others, mere teenagers. It prompted him to say, 'Cecilia, go sit next to him.'

She smiled, lowering her head. It was a pleasantly innocent sensation. Leopold prompted her again and this time she did as instructed. Though their ages betrayed them, the two could have been sitting on a bench at a 1950s doo-wop.

The wine was quickly consumed. And then another bottle. Leopold had been talking almost continuously, parading back and forth across his lounge room like a circus master. In a way, he was.

Abruptly, laidbackguy4 said, 'I think cunts are really mysterious.'

Leopold frowned, failing to find the younger man's meaning. Long-term marriage had eradicated any form of mystery for him.

Perhaps sensing her husband's hesitation, Cecilia almost belly-flopped onto the man, casting her arms around his neck, and began kissing him. The man was initially overwhelmed, but remembered that this was what he had wanted.

Leopold frowned again. His immediate thought was to drag his wife off the man and cast her to the floor. Yet this was what was supposed to happen. But it didn't feel like the way it was meant to. This was his fantasy after all. 'Ah, guys.'

She was only just settling in. She had to disentangle, though with some difficulty. 'Yes?'

'Remember me?' He heard his own words and realised how silly he sounded. The irony of it all. 'I mean, maybe it's time we head to the bedroom, before we get any more drunk. Ha ha.' His laugh was dry, a false echo of surety.

The younger man stood up.

Cecilia straightened her clothes, now eager. 'Sure. Let's go.'

Even though Cecilia was in a better position to view laidbackguy4's package, now more prominent, she didn't focus solely on it, instead aware of her husband's eyes on her. She found it difficult to control her breathing, overcome with potential thrill and expectant terror.

Leopold felt a surge of ownership and led the man down the hall into the bedroom, forgetting his wife, who brought up a slow third. 'Relax, you'll be fine,' said Leopold. 'Just pretend I'm not here.'

The man nodded uncomfortably, though he began unbuttoning his shirt.

Leopold looked around for his wife, realising he had forgotten her. 'Oh shit, there you are,' he said as she entered the room. 'You okay?'

She nodded but felt alone, abandoned, a bit player in a male world. Unappreciated, frightened, sick, excited. She had a strong urge to have the experience over with. She yearned for a new day. But first, there was this.

Her husband put his arm around her shoulder. 'You okay?"he repeated.

She straightened her back, immediately annoyed. 'I'm fine. Aren't you going to your chair?'

Flimsy silk scarves hung on each arm of the wooden chair situated in the corner.

'Yeah.' He went to it, his wife pressing at his back.

Laidbackguy4 sat on the edge of the bed, removing his shoes. 'You want some help?'

'No, she's fine,' said Leopold, annoyed at what felt like badgering.

Cecilia could sense her husband's anxiety as she carefully wrapped his wrists to the chair. She placed her face close to his, voice lowered, as though only they could hear. 'We can back out if you want.'

For a moment, he considered it. 'No. I'm fine.'

'Are you sure?'

He grinned, but it was fictitious. 'How about you? You sure?'

'I will be if I know you are.'

'I'm not here, remember? I'm the cuckold one.' He raised his voice and peered around his wife's hips. 'I'm the cuckold!'

The younger man double blinked. 'Cock. Old?'

'Cuckold. You know, cuckold? I'm the bastard who doesn't know.'

'Oh, right,' the man conceded, though was lost. He placed his jeans on a folded pile on the floor with the rest of his clothes. He stood upright in his bright blue briefs, aware of his taut, younger body, suddenly stuffed with inspiration.

Cecilia kissed her husband on the forehead and turned to face the other.

Leopold felt her lips long after the kiss. It bothered him. He wished he could remove it, wipe his skin, but didn't want to lose the feeling of being unable to move. Even with a little force he could free himself. He wasn't sure why it was playing on his mind so much. Maybe it was due to the condescending way she had kissed his head, like a good little boy. Or maybe because it was all so polite and with his consent. It was supposed to be deceitful and secretive.

He had tried to capture this unique feeling in his twenties, experimenting. It had begun with a strip club. Once he generated the courage, provided by alcohol, he requested a private dance. Though an enlightening experience, it didn't sit comfortably with his imaginings and he never did it again. The young woman had been too conscious of him, had made too much effort to please him. He couldn't trust her motives. That's why he knew he could never find satisfaction from a working girl and had never engaged one. He knew where many (really only one) of his fantasies had come into existence, though he did not want to acknowledge it as it seemed too simplistically Freudian.

He believed his childhood experiences were based more on his already formed, albeit immature, voyeuristic tendencies. While not yet eleven, he was able to spy on his sister getting changed, usually straight after a shower as she walked towelled and dripping from the bathroom to her bedroom. There was a gap in her bedroom curtains, though he suspected she left it partially open on purpose. She was studied in awe from Leopold's bedroom, by gazing at the strategically placed, though cracked, hand mirror placed in the overgrown garden. Though she still annoyed him no end, she possessed a power that made him jealous and angry. She was a thing of spectacle and wonder, grown from who knows where. He knew it was wrong to look upon her, felt the sin through his core. The more he tried to stop himself, the longer he lingered by the window. This went on for around fourteen months until, at the age of sixteen, she took up a boyfriend who would come over after school. She began hanging a sheet in between her bedroom curtains, which ruined any more viewings. Leopold could still visualise plenty, especially with an ear to the wall. In fact, the more she attempted to disguise her behaviour, the more he desired to be witness to it.

By the time he was a young man, he was significantly ashamed of his adolescent actions and did his best to forget them. Yet watching his wife sitting on the edge of the bed and fondling the cock of another man, it did more than remind him of those days. It was like being inside his sister's bedroom. And that wasn't necessarily a good thing.

Laidbackguy4 slid to a squatting position on the floor. He seized

Cecilia by the hips like a thing made only of sex and pulled her forward. Her feet went instinctively up onto his shoulders, like she once did with her husband, before he became complacent.

Leopold had the best seat in the house, literally, but his forehead still twitched from where she had kissed him. He couldn't scratch it. He also needed to pee and regretted not pre-empting it earlier. He had been too busy trying to be the big man. Now he was dizzy from too much wine and needed water. He would set it up differently next time. If there was a next time. His wife was moaning. He was pretty certain that she didn't moan that loudly for him. In fact, he was positive.

'Oh, my God,' said laidbackguy4. 'You're pretty wet.'

'That's your fault,' she said with a giggle.

Leopold's face morphed colour to a patchy crimson. Did she need to be so girly? His wife was enjoying it just a bit too much. And she knew that he knew.

'Jesus,' said laidbackguy4. 'I could drown here.' He laughed.

'I'll throw you a life jacket. Get on up here.' She looked to her husband. This was his idea. She added, 'With that big cock.'

The man rose. 'Yeah, baby.'

Cecelia moaned with wanton glee, as though it was to be her last time. 'For God's sake, just do it. Like Nike!'

In a blaze, Leopold ripped himself out of the chair, the scarves falling away.

Startled, laidbackguy4 stumbled to one side and, to prevent crashing onto the bedside lamp, lunged forward, prodding Cecilia in her stomach.

'Ooohhhh!' She rolled away and coughed, partially winded.

Leopold launched himself at the naked man on the bed, fists flying.

Laidbackguy4 tried to scuttle away, squirming back to the bedhead, away from his attacker and in a better strategic position. He lashed out with his heel and cracked Leopold on the cheek. He brought his foot back, ready to catapult again but Leopold was slipping down the bed to the floor, not unconscious, but in resignation, a silent retreat. His hand went to his face. He knew something was fractured if not broken.

Cecilia rolled back, taking in air and examined the bizarre sight before her. She too had heard the crack, but wasn't certain who or what the sound belonged to. Until now. 'Stop,' she said rather softly to laidbackguy4, his foot still parked mid-air, revealing his shaved sphincter (bum Brazilian?).

He had not moved for some seconds, like an amateur attempt at an exotic wood carving.

Cecilia slipped to the floor where her husband now sat and began to check his face. Leopold was squinting, his right eye watering above his split cheek.

Laidbackguy4 rolled from the bed and went to retrieve his clothes. Unfortunately, Leopold was sitting on some of them. He tried to signal to Cecilia to help him but she simply said, 'See what you've done? Just get out!'

He pointed. 'But…my clothes.'

Cecilia looked down. Leopold was sitting on the jeans.

'Oh, honey. Um…'

But Leopold was too deep within himself to comprehend.

She tugged on the jeans but they could only move so far. 'Ah, honey, you have to get up.' She attempted to push Leopold off but he only groaned. She got to her feet and yanked hard on the jeans and Leopold tilted like a bowling skittle. The jeans flew out and Cecilia fell back onto her naked butt with a thud.

She sat there stunned, her bum throbbing, perhaps heralding a bruise. How was this happening? There was a half-naked stranger in their bedroom, holding his shoes, with his hand out to her, his impressive penis so close yet so far. She held up his jeans and he took them.

'Thank you,' he whispered.

'No worries,' she said as calmly as a bakery attendant.

Later, she couldn't fathom how she had been so polite to the man who had caused so much fuss. And yet, it hadn't been his fault. It was her husband's. Hers too, for secretly wanting the encounter. On the other hand, there was some regret. She never got to try out that weapon. She bet it could pack an almighty punch.

It was the end of their online escapades and it seriously quelled Leopold's long-cultivated fantasies. Decades had dissolved in seconds. Every time henceforth, when he caught himself returning to his imaginings, along came its inexorably linked cousin, the Chauceresque bedroom farce.

The world can be a chaotic place, especially in the boudoir, where strangers fear to tread. And for good reason.

The Fence Sitter

I am young in my head. But sometimes I feel old. Such as now. Walking past the local shops. Every step's a struggle. People pass me in a hurry and I think, why? It's just another day.

There's nothing wrong with taking your time. If there was something in my way, I'd probably bump into it. Or someone. I've done that too, because I never know which way to go. Left or right? A sumo wrestler's shuffle. They're just as much to blame but I'm the one they get annoyed with. They think I'm some mad old coot. Get out of the way, you stupid man.

If you're over sixty, you should be talked down to. Disregarded. Maybe it's my clothes. I'd buy a new set if I could afford to. Or maybe it's my face. People are quick to judge others based on their looks. We haven't come very far in five million years. Not in all ways. I guess in some ways. And strike me sideways, I've walked straight past the newsagent. Always doing something like that. Stuck in my head. God help me if I ever get a busy life again. Not likely. Not busy. No way. So I don't need your help after all, God. Okay with you?

I make out like it was my intention all along to turn round and head into the shop. Have to be seen to be in control. No one trusts you if you hesitate. Took me far too long to understand that. Still, I think deliberation is misunderstood.

Once inside, I'm immediately distracted by the face of the attractive young girl behind the counter. And doesn't anyone under forty look young now? I guess she's really not a girl at all, but a woman. She doesn't look at me. I'm not old enough to get the automatic pleasantries afforded to the elderly. As though all old people are nice.

I'm really not that old but the point is, I feel like it. I'm past it. I'm not tired of being alive, but I'm tired of living. If that makes sense. Tired of menial tasks like this, to fill the day. I pick up the paper.

I pay for it with barely a glance from her. She sees me often enough but doesn't say anything. Not that I say anything either, but I'm the one handing over the money. Hell, I've got what I came for. I'll go back and read it slowly throughout the day. Make it last. As though I care that much about what's going on. I've been around long enough to see it all. Everything's cyclical. Decade in, decade out. The same people, governments, unions, armies, countries, doing the same old shit to each other. Nothing ever changes. Only you do, as you shift up the rungs of ageing. And become the stereotype you swore you'd never be.

The sky is darker. I think it's going to be a day indoors, with the rest of the 'unwanted', my fellow boarding house drifters. United we fall, divided we may just survive. We may board there but it's definitely no home in the sense that most think of home. It's a bed and a cupboard and, my God, you better keep that room locked, even if you're in it. Especially if you're in it.

I return to the pedestrian crossing. Yet I'm the one who must wait for the cars. Most will stop but plenty don't. I stopped getting angry at those selfish arseholes a long time ago. There will always be arseholes, especially when they're cocooned from the world in their vehicles, just as there will always be greed and corruption and drunks and teachers and do-gooder religious types who are only trying to double their odds into the Promised Land. I gave up on religion way back. Sounded too good to be true. And if it sounds it, it probably is. All that devotion rubbish. You never get anything back. It's like continuously paying for a pizza that never turns up. Still, you can't rule out the Big Fella. Not completely. So I throw a prayer out there occasionally, just to keep a toe in.

A ute sneaks through the crossing, but the next car, a black four-wheel drive, eases to a standstill. I walk onto the crossing, deliberately slow, drawing out the frustration so they can curse me, the old bastard. I was once in a hurry too. Rush rush to nowhere. It doesn't make sense to punish the person who stopped for me, I know, but I can't punish the arsehole who didn't. Life isn't righteous, but I didn't create the rules.

I have two and a half blocks to walk. Most days, I take my time and pretend to admire the houses. How I used to love having my own house. Naturally, I didn't appreciate it then. Probably moaning about some arsehole I had to work with. Or the neighbour. I shouldn't be so glib. I'm glad I'm still here. I've seen many go over the years. People who deserved more. While the dickheads linger. And that's part of nature's joke. Let your guard down and that's when you fall down. Literally fall over, due to some protruding concrete because someone couldn't be bothered to call the council and, if they did, the council couldn't be bothered to fix it. It's a funny old world. You must remain vigilant. Because someone could short change you with a smile and maybe it was an accident and maybe it wasn't. And maybe I'll go on living and maybe I'll drop dead tonight.

I think I think too much. Do I? Maybe I delude myself too. And maybe I debate with myself too much and maybe those grey black clouds have rain in them and maybe they don't. And maybe this girl coming towards me will cross the road to avoid me, because that happens, or maybe she'll put her head down or look straight ahead like a robot and pretend I don't exist and by doing so, actually validate my existence. Because God forbid it's too much to ask to smile at a stranger.

Let's wait and see what she does. Maybe I'll look at her. Okay, I'm going to stare. She'll think I want her. That I'm some dirty old perv because only the young are entitled to hormones. Only the young are allowed to be human. She's all of twenty-five. With that self-righteous swagger. Well, let me tell you something, missy, I can still rise to the occasion, on occasion. But if it were to happen, in a pressure situation like that, could I? Not a hope. But once I could. She'll either look straight down, say seventy per cent, or straight ahead, thirty. Closer now. Now, I'm not sure. Fifty-fifty? She looks at me. Shit. I'm wrong. I'll give her a smile because I feel bad for staring. Oh-oh, she's turned the frown on. Quickly becoming a sneer. Here she is.

'Hello,' I say. 'I think it's going to rain!'

'Dirty old pedo,' she mumbles and passes me.

I get a waft of too much perfume. My stomach drops and I instantly feel depressed. I stop and watch her. I've never seen her before but she has destroyed me with three words. How is that possible? I feel like scum. I am scum. She has a nice derrière, though. A little big but I can live with that. Oh, Jesus. Perhaps she's right. Though I was only talking about the weather.

It is going to rain. Can I not look at someone passing me in the street? Is she invisible? Are we supposed to pretend in a city full of people that we're not really here? God forbid we should acknowledge one another. After all, there are serial killers on every corner. And those rapists are always clogging up the supermarket queues. What did she call me? A pedo? But isn't she a grown woman? I must have missed something. Maybe I am old.

She looks back over her shoulder, still with the curled lip, as though I've actually committed some disgusting crime. I guess I shouldn't have looked at her. I've obviously made her feel uncomfortable. I didn't mean to. Oh, dear God, I'm sorry about that. Am I a terrible person? Or was she just a bitch? I suppose it doesn't matter. She'll have her impression of me and if she ever sees me again, I'll be that creep. No matter what. Maybe I'll have to buy one of those priest collars. Then she'll be the one to feel bad. Then again, some of those priests ain't too saintly either.

I begin walking again, slower this time. I don't care if the heavens open up. Heaven. If that's what Heaven's like, it must be a wet dark place. Truth is, I was never very good with the ladies. Not at forty, or thirty or twenty. Maybe at twenty-seven or twenty-eight for an interlude, as if to show me what I was missing out on. But then it was taken away.

They say it's better to have lost than to have never had. I don't agree. You know what you're missing out on. The harder I tried, the more elusive they became. I attempted to learn the art of seduction. I studied movies, bought books and made a fool of myself more often than I've had hot breakfasts. And I don't eat breakfast.

I wasn't without some charm, but I lacked confidence. Women can see through it, like one-way glass. I guess I wasn't good-looking enough. Women, men too, will excuse any shitty behaviour from a looker. That's why I went through that whole bitter stage. God, that lasted more than ten years. Maybe twenty. I had to let it go in the end or I would have gone nuts. Too much thinking. It's like you're only allowed so many thoughts in a lifetime and if you use them up too quickly, it sends you barrelling down the loony chute. What a waste of good years. It wasn't worth it. They're not worth it.

There was Carol of course. She was all right on the eye. Not great but I wasn't going to look a gift horse in the mouth. Especially since I don't like horses. Their mouths are weird. The beginning was great. Fell hook line and sinker. Mainly because I didn't know her then. Still, I got a taste for it. And that's what kills. I soon worked out that she was as mad as a hatter.

I got rid of her. I thought it would be easy to get another. I was so wrong. I tried to get Carol back. By then she was with some other poor bastard. I think I was only after the sex. She was great in the cot, tears and all. That's the mad ones for you.

Months became years, became decades. So I let it go and focused on my happiness. I had to. Maybe I just gave up. Probably a mistake in hindsight. All those years alone. But hey, I still have me. What's so bad about being alone? Why are we made to feel like there's something wrong with us if we are? I chose this way. My way or the highway. You know what? It takes a lot of guts to live by yourself. Guts. Yeah, I know I've got a beer belly. Very funny. Can't see my toes when I'm pissing. Ha ha.

There's always some joke designed for somebody. Made at their expense. Hey, I was only joking! Rotten bastards. Every place I ever worked. The clothes store, the cigarette joint, the RSL, the park job, the bus depot and the rest. Always some smart-arse. Some people weren't too bad but they were never around long enough. Just in and out. Get what they want. I don't know. Maybe it was my fault too. I never knew what to say. But I'd had enough.

Don't read me wrong. I'm not a bloody fence-sitter. I'm not boring. I just don't run around shooting my mouth off to impress people like other dickheads. I mean, you've got to take the good with the bad, but do I have a sign around my neck saying, make me the target of all your second-hand shitty jokes? And while you're there, make me the bloke who doesn't get promoted too. Even though I'm busy working while everyone else is talking shite. Make me the bloke who drifts from job to job. Make me the bloke who doesn't get the girl. Make me the nervy guy who got old and can't work any more. Make me the bloke who has to live in a bloody boarding house because I can't afford to live anywhere else.

And maybe I'm feeling sorry for myself again. I feel pathetic. I hate what the mirror reveals. Sometimes I don't give a crap because somebody's got to look after me. And now it's going to rain after all. Hell and damnation. Well, I'm too old to run. I'm not going to. In fact, I'm going to stop right here and get wet. I'll be determined for once. And that sky's black and mean and strike me down if it isn't going to bucket down like my old grandma's slop bucket. Let it come. What do they say now? Bring it on, mother-fucker. I'm going to get totally wet and my paper's going to be ruined but it's too late. It's only water, right? I'll stand up to it. I'll stand up to the Heavens if it's really up there instead of running like always.

Running from those jobs because it got too hard or because some bastard gave me a hard time, just like it was in school. Or running away from the girls because I was worried they'd reject me and I should have just gone for it because it's too bloody late now and I'm not even left with any decent memory except for kooky Carol to flog over and all I've got is my wet clothes and the rain on my head which drips into my eyes.

I throw the sodden paper to the pavement. I don't give a shit any more. I'm going to walk out onto the road. It's not that busy but if a car does come, I'm not going to move. If they want to run me over, they bloody well can and do me a favour because I don't have the guts, ha ha, to do myself in, but I'm standing up for myself. For once.

I'm on the road and it's pelting down and I hope to God they come right now because I'm ready. I see some lights because the day has turned to night like it's angry and wants to hurt somebody. I'm staying firm in my position. This is what I should have done years ago.

There's water and wind and streaks and noise and the lights are big and I wonder if they can see me and they're not going slow, not as slow as they should be in this horrendous weather so it must be some arsehole and maybe they won't see me and maybe I should move out of the way and maybe I'm being a stupid old bastard, crazier than Carol. I could be back in my room dry and warm on my bed but maybe it really is time to make a stand and God's probably watching to see if I have the stomach for it and there's a lock of brakes and a sliding screech and I don't know who I'm talking to, me, the driver or God but all I've got time to yell is, 'I didn't mean it!'

Did I?

My Daddy Used To Say…

I gotta be quick, as my girlfriend's just gone out and she doesn't think I'm the writing type, and I'm not I guess. But as my daddy used to say, son, be true to who you are. Ha ha. I always wanted to say, my daddy used to say… It sounds like from a movie or song, but of course, my dad never said shit. The whole time I knew him. Up until I was fifteen and two-thirds. I wasn't given any of that guidance crap. He was an arsehole. Okay, so he never hit me, only that one time when I was eleven when he lost it after a fight with Mum and pushed me against the door as he stormed out. He was so withdrawn and hardly ever showed emotion so, you know, I suppose you could call it a form of abuse. I don't want to dishonour his memory, whatever the hell that means. I wouldn't say this to anyone and no one will ever read this except me, but he never really talked to me, like you'd expect a dad to do. Like a boy needs.

So yeah, I did join him on some of his walks and he gave me a few tips about the dangers of nature and stuff of that nature (yep, I'm not the writing type ha ha), but Mum never understood that it wasn't enough for me. She thought, still thinks, that I was too harsh on Dad, unfair when he can't defend himself. She's still protecting him over me, even though he's dead. Apparently I'm being selfish. She doesn't understand me. I'm not attacking him anyway. I'm just telling it how it is. Was.

Anyway, I don't get along all that great with her but my brother does. He's five years younger and doesn't have the same issues as me. And he's a mummy's boy. Okay, it's closer to four but I was a teenager and he wasn't. It makes a difference. I mean, I don't blame my drinking on my dad. I like to drink. It makes me happy, not sad or angry not like some people who can't handle their booze. I'm not hurting anyone, so what does it matter?

My girlfriend thinks it matters, but it doesn't. Obviously tonight she had to drive to the supermarket for the toothpaste instead of me, even though we could have gone without for one night. Usually my drinking's not a problem, except when she decides to make it one. Why does she have to do that? Why do women do that? She busts my chops a lot. I work. I earn money. I don't hit her or swear at her. I only swore at her when I used to defend myself, like a man should, but now I don't bother. It's over more quickly if I just let her carry on a bit. Okay, more like a lot. She's like one of those old dolls where you pull the string and it cries. Waaah waaah waaah. She's actually worse now, on account of me being a father soon. Yeah, I know. I shouldn't let her go out at night being pregnant and all. Thirty-one weeks. Not sure how many months that is. Of course I didn't want her to go, but she's so stubborn! She was trying to making a point. Like if something happened to her, it'd be all my fault. As I said, women, I don't get them.

Besides, it's not going to stop me from drinking. I can be a good dad. And I know I will be. My dad's drinking wasn't a problem. It was to Mum, though. She would carry on about it to him but not to me. I had other things to deal with later, I guess, not so much at the time. These things tend to develop as you get older. When you grow up, you realise stuff that you just didn't notice as a kid. I feel like I didn't really know who he was. Just this quiet man who liked to work, walk and drink. I suppose he was a decent guy, but who really knows what he was thinking?

Okay, I've had my rant. Maybe I'll throw this out eventually, like the last one. Better go before the wifey comes back. Wife to be. The ball and chain. Ha ha. Don't get me wrong. I love her and all, but part of me doesn't want to let her get too close, you know? I'll give her what she wants but this is my life too. I gotta save something for me. Why should you give up everything for another person? There's a part of you that no one should touch. No one can know what's in your head anyway, and that's fine with me.

To be honest, I'm really not that great at expressing myself. I might write it, but if you ask me, talking is overrated. Words don't always cut it. So I keep them to myself. That's just the way I am.

Thirteen Steps: Living on a Stair

Chuu arrived home with his insignificant earnings from a day spent begging. Life had never been easy but, due to the current state of the nation, never this bad. He refused to allow his two children, Katsumi, twelve, and Kan, seven, to beg with him, although they stood a good chance of increasing his potential for gain.

He entered the three-storey house through a side entrance, bypassing the door to the owner's floor. She was a most unpleasant woman who would not give them a shred of extra space unless they could come up with more money. It was fine for the five renters of the bottom floor, all academics over the age of fifty. One of them was employed and they looked out for one another. Yet Chuu was proud and if his family had to live on the stairs, so be it. At least the steps were carpeted, even if they were as worn as his decade-old jacket.

His wife Asami greeted him. They kissed. He handed over a meagre palm's worth of coins. Once again, he felt the guilt bubble inside him. He had met her on a cleaning job, some fourteen years before. He had promised her a better life. Having two children, in hindsight, may have been a mistake, but no one could have foreseen the far-reaching economic turmoil to come. She sighed. All he could do was lower his eyes.

The second floor was indeed empty, yet the demon upstairs refused to allow the family of four to inhabit any part of it. Unless something changed soon, they were set to remain on the stairs indefinitely.

He gave a little wave to his daughter, who occupied the bottom three steps. Being twelve was tough and her return wave lacked enthusiasm. The next three steps belonged to young Kan. The parents shared the top six steps. The boy grinned and scrambled to his father, who picked him up, gave him a quick cuddle and was put down again. The boy was growing.

The uppermost step, the thirteenth, was multi-purposed. Sometimes Katsumi was sent there as punishment, but she liked the view. She could look down on her parents. It made her feel superior. Lately, she found herself agitating them for no apparent reason. Despite knowing the answer, she asked her father if he had earned much for the day. Chuu told her not to be disobedient, that it wasn't his fault that the country had gone bad. She turned away from him.

Asami knelt and put the coins in a leather pouch, muttering that it wasn't enough, that if it wasn't for Aki, the most senior of the academics, they might actually starve. Chuu grew despondent. It was the same old argument but he would not hear of charity. Asami said that she was happy to work for the academics, if he would only relent on his pride. Chuu stamped the step. He was the head of the family. He knew best. Asami said he should be thinking of the children. He replied with vigour that it was all he thought of. He reminded her of his plan, but they had to be patient.

The truth was, he had no plan other than to steal, which he had so far avoided as he was an honourable man. Besides, theft had become more prevalent in society and, therefore, much harder to accomplish. Yet he would not admit defeat. His pride was all he had left.

The next day, a Sunday, while Chuu was out, Asami crept down the second staircase, a decaying spiral to the academics' door. She knocked. It took some time for it to open. The academics accessed their floor from the rear of the building and so were not used to the door being used. Luckily for her, it was Aki. The others were not as kind, the well of human kindness not being as deep as it once was, seemingly in line with economics. He invited her in.

She told him she would happily cook for them during the day, as long as her husband did not find out. Aki replied that the academics liked cooking but concurred that they detested cleaning. There was a murmur of dissent amongst the others but Aki was insistent. She set immediately to task, dusting with a disused shirt from the youngest professor. Nothing was thrown out any more and here was justification in motion. The four men sat and watched her with mystification. It had been a long time since there had been a female in their midst, not including the upstairs owner, who was about as palatable as the second-rate (some said fabricated) seaweed, which was everywhere these days in lieu of meat and vegetables.

When Chuu arrived home, he was surprised to see extra food lined up on step twelve, the pantry and cooking area. He asked where it had come from. Asami told him. Chuu thundered into a fury. Kan scuttled down to his sister's domain, step two, where they huddled. When father became angry, all of Japan knew about it. After some time, as Asami was no push over, the anger fell out of Chuu. He could not deny his children the extra food. He was losing control. And he knew it.

That night, he found it difficult to tell his story, too distracted by the shift his family were taking. Most nights he would enlighten them with adventures of his day and those from his past, before he met Asami. Naturally he would embellish these stories. And yet he had neglected to tell his wife that when he was a boy, he had witnessed a man break into their home and, finding his mother alone with her only child, rape her. Chuu had never forgotten his mother calmly asking her attacker if she could send her child out of the room lest he witness it. The intruder granted her this request.

Much later, Chuu realised the significance of this act, the sacrifice his mother had made in order to protect him. His mother died less than a decade later and he never had the opportunity to speak to her about it in any detail. The memory had shaped his adult self. He had to protect his family, even if it meant that they went hungry. He would not allow his children out onto the street. Of course Katsumi resented him for not allowing her to go to school, yet her mother did her best to provide a basic education. Schooling on step ten.

Two days later as Chuu walked the frigid, grey streets, he found he could not stop thinking about his wife, the only woman he had ever loved, save his mother, surrounded by those haggard, white-bearded strangers, who he thought were probably ogling her. He rushed home. He opened the door and was struck with a terrifying yet exhilarating thought. He could break into the owner's floor, kill her and move his family into the space. Would anyone miss the demon witch? Kill? Where had that thought come from? What sort of example would that be to his children?

He went directly to the stairs. Asami was already there. He pressed her for information. She only provided him with a perfunctory explanation as to her day's events. Katsumi gave him a cheeky look, as though she enjoyed his suffering. He asked her if she knew anything. The girl turned away. Asami reprimanded him. She said it would continue until Chuu could come up with a better solution to their woes.

That night, on stair ten, he found restlessness constant. He could no longer hide his suspicions. He woke his wife. He quietly asked her if she was performing furtive acts for food. She denied it. He asked if the grey ones were pressuring her into anything she did not want to do. After all, men were filthy rats.

Katsumi overheard much of what was said, though pretended to be asleep. It solidified her own suspicions of the sexual nature of human beings. She was all too aware of the changes in her own body. The next day, when Kan was doing his homework (counting the carpet fibres on step four), she took a chance and quizzed her mother over what she had heard.

Her mother had known that this day would come, but felt disheartened that the conversation of the adults, a rather inappropriate one in her mind, had hastened her daughter's inquisitiveness. This further brought on feelings in herself that had also been developing, those of discontent. Yet there were many families now living on the streets, which were not safe. As the owner had told them recently when the rent was late, there were others who would swiftly take their place.

While Asami realised that people can acclimatise to any situation, they also need to have a little hope.

The next day, Asami wanted to indulge a concept. She made a special effort, while cleaning, to bend over to test the reaction of the academics. In a way, it had been her husband who had secured the idea. Sure enough, they were all peering like naive, geriatric schoolboys. She knew she had them.

By the end of the following day, she had negotiated a new deal. She would clean for them, in her underwear, in return for a little cash in addition to the food. Her children knew nothing, relegated to the many tasks that she had set for them, reciting Japanese literature and poems taught through an old method re-employed, that of the oral tradition. They also had to exercise, repeatedly running up and down the thirteen steps. She understood that keeping the children occupied was necessary for their growth, physically and mentally. Yet these were desperate times. And that could only mean one thing.

Chuu remained despondent. His idea of eliminating the owner was not an option. Or maybe it was. There had to be a way out. His grip was slipping. His wife was now deliberately usurping him. After dinner he pleaded with her to give up the work. However, as she pointed out, unless he could provide an alternative, there was no point in quitting. They were eating much better than they had in the eight months they had been living on the stairs, with the potential to save money if they were guarded.

Chuu, unable to control his resentment, clamped his wife by the wrist and demanded that she give up her show for perverted professors. Katsumi yelled at him to stop. He let go, horrified that his child had witnessed his unsubtle attempt at coercion. He retreated to the top step, ashamed. He would have left the house entirely if not for the danger of the outdoors after dark and the possibility of abandoning his family to the whims of the academic degenerates.

Asami said that all would be fine if they kept their heads. They ought to be grateful for the extra portions that they were receiving.

She managed to placate him, but knew that dramatic change was inevitable.

Days became weeks. A tense, desolate balance found its way into the adult's relationship. Chuu wondered if the number of steps was a bad omen. The economic crisis had begun in the West. Perhaps their unlucky number thirteen had affected them too. He was certain something dreadful was going on, but Asami refused to discuss it.

Katsumi sat on step seven, staring at the tattered leather pouch on step eight. Her mother was away cleaning once more. How messy could those professors be? Katsumi had been instructed never to touch the pouch. Once, she would have obeyed her mother. Yet times had changed. Or perhaps she had. Her next actions would have consequences which she could never have foreseen, but she would find herself, in the years to come, returning to this particular instance. What might have happened had she let it be? The urge was too great. She opened the pouch.

There were many items inside; things she expected to find. Her mother's prayer beads, some old photographs, a few coins, expired make-up and an odd little device she had never seen before (a USB stick from another time). She groaned, disappointed. Remorse began to appear. She wished that she had never betrayed her mother's trust. She ensured that everything was put back as she had found it. She would instruct Kan not to tell.

As she was checking over the area, she spied a split in the carpet. It was a severed piece of fabric in the shape of a square. She lifted it. Underneath was a small bundle of money, a rare sight indeed. She brought forth a clump, discovering more beyond, shoved under the matting. At first she believed that she had made a miraculous discovery and couldn't wait to tell her parents. They would be proud. Yet, as she thought a little more, she became conscious of two things. One, that her mother had to have known about the slice of fabric with its prize, and two, that she would know that Katsumi had touched her mother's pouch. She put everything back the way she had found it, minus the cash.

She told her brother not to move, that she had to go and find their mother. Kan protested. His mother had given them strict instructions never to go downstairs. No. Matter. What. In case of an emergency, they had to go to the owner. The truth was that Kan had never been left alone. Katsumi held a finger to his face and said that if he moved, she would hit him. When their parents were away, she was leader. He sat back sulking, not wanting to let his sister know that he was spooked. He had a semblance of boyish pride after all, his father's son.

Katsumi scrunched the money into her pocket. She stood on the bottom step, worried that the floor might somehow swallow her up, even though she had seen her mother walk across it. It was time to be a grown-up. She took one small step. She waited. She was uninjured. And free. And yet her heart beat madly.

She spied the door leading to another set of stairs, an ancient, dark corkscrew. Light seeped from the bottom. It gave her the strength to enter. The steps were weak and crooked. She felt sorry for her mother, who had to navigate them twice daily. Katsumi crept. The wood whined. When she reached the bottom, she saw that the light came from beneath a rickety door with a golden knob, worn pale from the years. Over time, the door had lifted from the floor, leaving a gap. Shadows swam. There was activity beyond. She was jittery. She got down on her knees and placed her ear to the floor.

The first thing she noticed was the aroma of dust and the cool breeze that travelled along the floorboards. It made her eyes sting. Her next observations were problematic, as her sight was at a ninety-degree angle. It took some seconds for the ominous shapes to merge into identifiable people. In the middle of it all was her mother. She was naked. An elderly man stood behind her, also naked, holding onto her hips, moving slowly back and forth. There was another on the floor, his head between her legs. Yet another sat on a table, her mother's face in his lap. And one more rubbed her back like a slug. Katsumi wanted to scream for them to leave her alone but the horror was captive in her chest.

Her mother lifted her head, like a dog in a dirty alley. Did she know that Katsumi was there? Did she detect her pleading eyes beneath the door? Instead, she gave a perplexing moan. The girl was afraid that her mother was in pain until the man sitting down said something and she laughed with such vigour that Katsumi briefly wondered who she was.

The girl slowly retreated, mindful to maintain secrecy.

Roughly twenty-five minutes later, Asami collected a single note from each of the four men, excluding Aki. The fifth academic was not present, being the only one employed and who provided payment for his housemates' antics. Ironically, he was never able to take part. His recompense was that the others were required to treat him like an emperor, attending to his every whim. His only other request was that he not be spared any detail of his fellow academics' escapades.

Asami was pleased. She had not been required to clean for weeks and had accumulated enough funds to take her children away from the thirteen steps of misery in a pursuit of a better life. She would leave her husband behind. There was no choice. She could never explain to Chuu where the cash had come from. She could rent her own apartment. If need be, she could continue her new occupation while her children were at school. They had to come first, even before her husband. And herself.

She traipsed up the winding stairs, hopefully, for the last time. Yet when she returned, the children were nowhere to be seen. She searched in the bathroom, finding it empty. She approached the owner, who was belligerent but insisted she had not seen them. Terrified, Asami searched the surrounding streets. She was severed from her own flesh and blood. They had vanished. As she discovered later, so had all of her savings. She had only been doing what she thought best for her children and, in his own way, her husband as well.

Now the youngsters had flown the coop, no longer living on a stair. They had ascended.

I am. You were. He's not.

A story of shifting perspectives

First person

Not supposed to be a one-way street. Where the hell am I? Great map, assholes.

'Farrck!'

*

Second person

You are detached from the real world in such an all-pervading fashion, as though you have just been expelled from the womb, gasping for that first breath. You are cognisant of the face that you are injured, your blood-soaked sleeve a red flag, yet you stumble on. You are aware that you're walking down a street, or across or up as you're not sure as this is your first time in Minneapolis and the fresh vision of buildings and stores and other familiar entities that you had been so hungrily absorbing only minutes before now mean nothing. In fact, you retain no purpose or feeling, only the possession of a primal necessity that tells you to walk and keep on walking. Not to run or flee or expel unnecessary energy as your mind has already left your body and it matters not if you're here or there or back where you started some five-hundred-odd miles away. Despite what has happened, you do not wish to be home as you'd already had enough, though the image of your four-year (and four-month) year-old daughter waving goodbye, without being aware of what was truly happening ripped at your soul in a way no knife could duplicate. You do not feel regret because regret is an emotion and you have no need for them now. There should be relief that you have survived or perhaps fear that you may have unseen injuries or at least puzzlement as to what exactly took place, as that memory is not available in its entirety as though fragmented and dispersed like a deleted file that could possibly be reassembled, if only you knew where to look.

You know your name is Michael and that you are thirty-three years old and that you grew up in the country with two siblings, both much older, as you were a late addition and as a consequence were not close to them (not from your point of view) yet maintained a cordial relationship as you would to a respected uncle and aunt. You were mumma's boy but daddy's thorn and though your mother told you it was only because he was an older parent coupled with certain chemical changes which had made him a grumpy, silly man, you could never correlate this with how you felt or, more importantly, how he made you feel, which impacted acutely on your life, especially when he left you (and your mum) when you were thirteen, which only served to solidify those earlier suspicions.

When you were old enough, you moved into town, which was only twenty-three miles from your mum's home as you couldn't bear to leave her, though too independent to stay. She had wanted you to move upstate and follow your brother and sister's path and gone to university and become moderately successful, financially comfortable and therefore (in theory) happy, though you suspected it was all a sham, especially your sister, who was consistently if not permanently frustrated, bitter and hypersensitive while doting on you like her own child, which was not sentimental and endearing but controlling and patronising. You suspected that it could be your father's traits resurfacing in her, as your brother was also abrasive, but not all-pervading. He was also aloof yet insisted on maintaining the facade with his belief in the American dream, as he had the big house, two cars, three children, too many pets and a backyard pool, which meant nothing to you as you did not value materialism, which you proved by spending the crux of your twenties living off the seat of your pants, reading, drinking, fishing and watching movies, without really owning anything, even though you had decent employment in the town's only photographic store, producing average quality reprints of faded photographs and taking portraits of families who wished to lasso a forced moment as though one iota of a second represented the unit in totality to demonstrate to the world that they were happy and not the flawed dishevelled mess that constituted most families. You did not believe in love, peace and happiness and all that Hallmark bullshit, at least, not for you, not until you were twenty-seven and went camping with a buddy on the river and by the second night you were both so bored that you decided to drive out to the nearest tavern, where you became intoxicated and met Surfie Sam, as she was known, a twenty-two-year-old local who did, indeed, look like a surfer girl with faint dispersed freckles and sandy blonde hair, though she had never seen the ocean, much less mastered its complex patterns, but it was a title she preferred to Samantha.

In a few miraculous months, your world view changed and everything you thought you knew, particularly about yourself, sprouted inside out like petals in spring, revealing an inner depth and beauty that you never saw coming. Your mother and sister were very happy for you, though they spoke out against the hasty marriage. They were right of course, yet if you had your time over, you would have not replaced a minute. The only real regret you had was that by the time your daughter came along, you had realised that Surfie Sam was not your match and had been contemplating leaving but it wasn't right to abandon her, much less the child. You did not wish to be like your father, whom you did not see any more, which was more of a slow punishment as your father still sent the occasional email. You discovered the painful way (the only way?) that you cannot live forever on a promise, much less an ideal. The heart does as it wishes. Your patience for Samantha had an expiry date.

Third person

At the end of the day, he was a father and that could never be altered, even if he could not tolerate the day-to-day illusions of familial bliss, no matter what others might think. He was grateful to Sam, for now he knew that there existed a deep and true feeling like being witness to a new vibrant colour for the first time that was truly alive and wasn't merely a lie propagated by greeting card companies and florists and soppy films.

When he left, he felt guilty of course, coupled with a heaving sadness that crippled his legs and crushed his soul, yet he did have the rest of his life to consider and there was always the possibility that when he had re-established himself in the city, he could send for his daughter. He was imbued with hope and a little pride that he had finally disconnected himself from his past and was itching to see what lay in store. At least, he had been hopeful because now that was merely a word, like placate and railing and thermostat. There was nothing to attach to it. It was not void or empty. It was nothing.

He paused at the corner of Chicago Avenue South, ignoring the obvious stares from passers-by, and, for no reason at all, turned right and kept on.

Three Little Words

I'm an alcoholic. They make it sound so easy. So effortless, as though a simple admission makes everything okay. Kiss it better. All better now. Salvation through admission. Well, I'm not going to say it. I don't give in without a fight. I'm not your traditional run-of-the-mill drinker. Some talk about the daily battle with the booze. I think they've watched too many movies. Apparently alcos drink non-stop all day. If I did that, I'd be dead. I get hangovers like a shower of acupuncture needles, pain to the bone. You'd think it would be enough to make me stop. A day off and I'm back on it. I'm more of a casual drunk. For instance, I'm at the movies tonight, so I'm clearly not drinking. Tomorrow I will be. I have to. I do my best work when I'm half-cut.

I start late afternoon (could never fathom those morning drinkers), and start ringing around like crazy. After a couple of beers, I'm so confident that I can close deals in a fraction of normal time. Over the course of a week, I reach the same figures that others do, except I make most of mine in less than six hours. Two hours on the phone nursing beers in the bar and I go home satisfied. With work, that is.

I've got the taste by then. I need to keep churning. Ringing, running, burning, porning, wanking, passing out. Unlike the drunks in the movies, I don't leave a hurricane trail. I'm neat. I tidy up before bed. I drink water. I have to. Or I can't get up. I drink water all through the night. I still wake up feeling like shit. Must down two coffees before I can leave home. I pop painkillers all morning. I check emails and procrastinate. I don't talk to anyone if I can help it. I think they know. Most of them do. I don't care. I only care about me.

Some say alcoholics hate themselves. Why would I? I'm pretty cool. I'd hang out with me. I also care about my girl. Hence why I'm at the movies tonight, even though I'd rather be drinking. Occasionally I have to do something like this. I don't want her to think I can't have fun without booze. We haven't been together that long. She's a cute little number. I met her in the bar. Funny how that keeps happening to me. It's that confidence thing, you see. When I'm on fire, I can pick up the hottest woman within view.

If I get too drunk, though, I make a balls-up of it. I got beat up once because I was wasted. This little pocket rocket was with someone. I didn't notice. There's a downside sometimes. Three little words. Fuck you, man. I said that to his face. After he gave me a bleeding mouth. He came back and gave me another smack. I started drinking elsewhere after that. Can't win every time, right?

For some reason, though, the women don't last long. Can never figure them out. Not fully. I think they want the fairy tale. Well, life ain't no rom com, baby. It's more like a trashy soap opera on steroids. I can get 'em easy enough. And that's half the fun. There's always another one waiting around the corner, so who cares? Fuck them too.

Three words. They want intimacy. I'm not bothered. I impress 'em. I undress 'em. Ha ha. We go on a few dates. We fuck a while. I avoid them. I drink. They get insecure. We fight. Eventually they walk. Well that's life. Walk on by. Or drop in. Three little words. I may be a casual drunk but I'm still a winner. My world rocks. Hit me up. Pour me another. I'd tap that. Hey there, baby. You're the One. That's my line. Seal the deal. Or try to. I may lose. I may win. I'm an alcoholic. I don't care. Tomorrow's another day. And that's that.

Thanks for listening. Leave your number. If you're hot. Ha ha ha!

The First and Last Time

I made my first movie in 2009, *Down in the Dungeon*. It was special. Infamous, I guess. I never made another one for almost three months after that. It was a big deal. Not for some guys, but it was for me.

'Sorry. What was your name again?'

'Daz.'

'Right. Well, you just squat pretending to check out the dials like you're trying to work out what's wrong with it.'

'Shouldn't I have a spanner or something?'

'No. Just…push a couple of buttons. What's-his-name will come in.'

A voice from a short distance. 'Jim.'

'Whatever. He'll come in to stand over you, see what you're up to, then you look up and badda-boom-budda-baa. Start from there.'

'Um, so should I make the first move, or does he? What do I do?'

'I don't care how you do it. Just suck his dick.'

'Okay.'

'Then the cops will come in.'

'Ah, cop. We've only got one,' says another voice.

'Yeah, I know that. The cop will come in and arrest you for harassment.'

'Um, okay. But I'm confused. I'm the plumber and I'm in his house. Shouldn't they arrest him?'

'Do you want to be in the movie or don't you?'

'Sure. Yes.'

'Then you get arrested and put down in the dungeon. Like the title. Get it? Jesus. Just make it up as you go along, I don't care. No one cares.' He turns to the cameraman. 'Make sure we get plenty of visuals on the jizz shot.' He turns back to the actor. 'You know what directors say in this business? Make my day or no pay. So take it on the chin and make me grin. Now let's cock 'n' roll, people!'

It was tough. I mean, I wasn't expecting Scorsese or friggin' *Gone With the Wind* on the *Titanic* but I didn't expect everything to be so rushed. I gotta say, I did like being in front of the camera. And the money was good. It's what kept me going back. Not just the money. It's kind of good to have something under your belt, you know? An achievement… why are you laughing? Oh, I get it. Under the belt. It's okay to joke about these things sometimes. I get pretty down about what I've done, but I laugh too. It's not exactly a normal occupation, is it? Not that I expected it to become one. I had no idea it would take off like it did.

The company producer helped me a lot. 'Daz, listen, buddy. Stay with us, man. I'll make ya famous.'

'I'm not looking for fame. I just want to get a few titles behind me, get some money together, maybe achieve some personal goals, then get out.'

'That's what they all say.'

'Twelve months and I'm done.'

'Sure, Daz. I hear ya, man. I can help you achieve those goals. What do you want?'

'I don't know. I'm trying to prove something, I think.'

'You want money, right? I can get ya a great deal. Sign a contract, fifty movies or two years, whichever comes first.'

'Fifty? Jesus. I don't want to do that many.'

'Daz, my man. Stay with me. You're hot right now. We need ya. Who gave you your first break, huh? *Down in the Dungeon*.'

'I know and I appreciate it. Despite that dickhead director.'

'And I got rid of him for you, didn't I?'

'Yes, you did. But I need to be my own man. Besides, another twenty titles and I'm as good as done.'

Maybe I should've taken him up. I could have got the money up front and invested it. Instead of what I did, which was squander it on the good life and expensive presents for my girl. Oh, didn't I tell you?

I had a girlfriend. Pretty hot too. She dumped me. It wasn't because of the porn. It was…well…let's just say she was a fucking whore. Not an actual whore. She's a telemarketer. Phone job, like you. Very different to what you do of course. But it was funny how we met.

'You have the cutest voice.'

'Hee hee. Sir, you shouldn't…'

'Is the rest of you just as cute?'

'Maybe. Maybe not.'

'Well, I'd like to find out. Why don't I take you out for dinner?'

'Um, I'm not supposed to do this. We get recorded.'

'Come on. Live it up. I'm buying.'

'Okay then. Hee hee hee.'

I should have realised from the start. It was all about the money. She bled me like a freakin' surgeon, or one of those dead people dudes, who do you call them? Embalmers or whatever. She got me good. She was so little and hot. Big titties. Man, my dick's got me into a lot of trouble over the years. Kinda got me out of it too ironically. He earns the money after all. Maybe it's my brain that's fucked and my dick is the sensible one. I don't know…

Huh? Yes, I prefer girls. I wouldn't even classify myself as bi – that surprises you? Yeah, it does to most people. You know, I like sex. I'm good at it. Sex is sex, you know? I can focus on the physical actions and sensations. I like pleasing other people too. But I'm not attracted to guys. I don't look at 'em like that. I can appreciate a good body but…I look at girls. I love girls. I know. Weird, right? Who would have thought I'd end up being an adult star? If you'd told me that, even five years ago, I would called you nuts… How? Um, well… I met this guy at a mate's barbecue and he got me in. Simple as that. A chance meeting, I s'pose. Life's very strange sometimes.

Um. Yeah, look, I don't want to go into too much detail about that, okay? You don't know who these people are connected to. I mean, it's not some movie Mafia drug thing going on. I mean, it could be but as far as I know everyone was legit. They're a little weird but I used to work in retail and, oh my god, every third customer was fucking nuts, you know what I'm saying? It's just best not to talk about it. Call it professionalism or whatever. I know it seems strange talking about discretion when I've got my dick flapping in the wind on some DVD. You can still order my titles if you want. Check out *My Big Fun Greek Orgy*, that's a good one. *Harry Plugger and the Philosopher's Boner.* Um, *The Anal Avengers.* Oh and *When the Balls Toll.* Classic. The rest were crap. You don't know what you're getting into until you're into it. Know what I mean? And no, you dirty prick, I'm not talking about being balls deep in butt. I mean the films. But that's the job. It's not as much fun as it looks.

Money? Yes and no. I had other issues going on. My mum had not long died. I wasn't in a good way that year. Or even before then. I get depression. Obviously. My mum was sick for a long time. She just couldn't shake it. It was a big drain on all of us, but being the youngest, I looked after her the most. I know in most families the oldest carries the burden, but not us. Look, I don't want to sound like a whiny cunt, sorry, like a whiner, I was happy to do it. I love my mum but, you know, I've always had my own issues. I've never really had a career or family of my own. My siblings think they're more important than me. Seriously, they're selfish. Of course they were at the hospital and Peter, that's my brother, was talking to the doctors like he was the main one. Arsehole. Same at the funeral. Had to be a big dick. And everyone fussing over my sister because she was bawling like a baby. Please. I reckon half of it was her guilt coming out.

Anyway, I don't care about that any more. I hardly talk to them these days. That was…shit…seven years ago? I never would've had a career in porn if Mum was alive. No way. I think part of it was revenge. On the others. On the world. I shocked a lot of people. I don't talk to anyone from those days any more. I don't care. I'm glad. But at times, I miss having someone to talk to. If I had a friend to talk to about my shit, maybe I would've been okay. Maybe.

Anyway, listen… I'm whining here… I know it's your job, but

I'm a sooky bitch. That's what Peter used to call me as a kid. I was. I mean, I am. I get down and I express myself. People think I do it for attention. They thought my porn stint was for attention. Fuck them. I did it for the experience. I've regretted it at times of course, like when Carmilla dumped me. She found out. That's because I was stupid enough to leave one of my DVDs in the cupboard. She was a bitch anyway, searching through my shit. What's wrong with people? I'm sick of them. Aren't you? I bet you get sick of people ringing up and crying woe is me all the time. I should probably let you go… No, I'm okay. I'm not going to do anything stupid. I mean, I'm still going to kill myself but what I call doing something stupid is like those people who go ape shit and hold someone hostage or stab someone or go on a wild cop chase and kill some innocent fucker, you know? I'll do it in my own time. Nice and quiet, no fuss. Just to prove to Peter and Jenny and the rest that I didn't make a big charade out of it. A final little finger up at them…

Counselling? With them? Are you serious? No fucking way. I wouldn't give them the satisfaction. They lost it with me years back. Therapy? What for? I'm perfectly clear in my head. Listen. I'm beyond all that now, don't you see? It's too late for girlfriends and friends. It's too late for family. I'm done.

Really? Who are you to tell me what I should do? I don't like fucking therapists or counsellors or any of those smug cunts. They charge too much and pretend to care when they don't give a shit! They laugh behind your back and the next time you go in they've got this smug arse face. Fuck them!

I don't want to calm down. I like being angry. Get your own life instead of worrying about everyone else's! You're no better than those misery sucking therapists… Calm down? Wow, the cheek. You know, you're a real dickhead. I don't know why I told you anything about me. You can go and get fucked!

Island of Jonas

As Jonas stood on the dock, disembarking passengers in a swirl of semi-chaos around him, he had no idea what the future would bring, let alone the next few hours. The island was tourism-based but his intention was to stay. And to forget. Leave the questions behind. Especially the biggest question of all: why? An exercise in futility, he knew. Yet he laid his hopes on the distance he had created.

Gilded by sand. Sparse of souls. Within an hour, he realised his own company made him feel…crowded. The distance did not alleviate his pain. At all.

Settling into the hut with the ocean view, the bamboo walls were already stifling. He tried to find solace in the natural state of things. The caressing winds that carried the smell of the ocean. The sounds of the rush of the tide against the shore. The way the light gave radiance to the trees. As though trying to convince himself that life was all around him (still) and was as majestic as he had once found it. The leaves swayed to the tone of the breeze. Their song everlasting. And the sand was as soft and crunchy beneath his feet, as it had always been.

And yet he knew instinctively that no matter how long he remained on the island, none of these things could redeem him. They had lost all meaning. The natural elegance of the tropics was as murky as the repetitious London streets he had left behind.

Two weeks in, he had cabin fever, despite spending more time outside than he had in a year at home. He embarked on a walk, a quick one, in order to calm himself. As the dusk settled, bringing with it his need for the deadening effect of his alcoholic medication, he observed a bird flailing on the ground in the shade of a tropical fern. Its colours were immaculate, yet its pain exquisite. A damaged beak, a broken wing – lost in flight, he speculated, crashed into a branch, deceived by a trick in nature, perhaps a flash of light. Yet also the victim of its own failings. It wasn't to know that life could also betray.

He could not look away. He searched his thoughts for a solution, already knowing that there was nothing he could do to save it. The parallels struck him. While his own ailments were not physical, he was perhaps worse off than this creature. It wanted to live. And it was only in this moment, as he watched its doomed struggle by his feet, that he comprehended his fate. His own struggle was pointless. He could not turn a metaphysical corner. His wife would forever remain below ground, a decaying husk. There was no redemption to be found. His shortcomings as a practitioner of medicine had failed her. His pride had interjected into her need for more professional care. Worst of all, she had trusted him.

He immediately knew what had to be done for the bird. And then for himself. Both had been deceived by the deficiencies of their own instincts. A decision, culminating with the taking of a life. Both casualties in life's endless, sporadic acts of cruelty.

He scooped up the bird and dashed its head against the earth. And left the ants to do the rest.

Her waterfall tears. Her watershed moment.

VI

She stepped onto the rock. Judged the distance to the next. Followed through. Rocks half-submerged like a trail of broken walnuts. Contemplated. Manoeuvred the fringe of the stream. Placing Him behind her. Something inside had switched. Yet thrust forward. An emotive conveyor belt. Perhaps it was her age. Perhaps a new determination. Emotional as she was, she was somewhat detached. Able to purvey. She was often successful at navigating her way through various obstacles, the issues of her teenage life. Hop. Step. Leap. Dry rocks. Tree branches. Moss. The water sucked the heat from the air. Her exposed legs cool. Shorts. T-shirt. Cropped, mousy hair. Sweat peas on brow. Tears pushing. Persistent. This time, she keeps them at bay.

V

The mist greeted them. Granules massaging skin. Ephemeral touches. A coalescing fog. A polite roar of water, giving in to space before crashing onto rocks, perpetually wet. Clusters of tourists rushed to seize the moment with a photograph, as though the cascade were in danger of instantly drying up. Captured. Savoured oh so briefly, some not at all, before moving on. The couple were not so different. He shot off a photo of her silhouetted against the murky white bush. She could not generate a smile. She took a shot of him. He beamed. He wanted one together. She declined. She moved to the edge where the rocks met the rainforest and found a place to sit.

He watched her. Sighed. Stared at the water for a time. Not

searching for a solution, merely a moment of sedateness before the inevitable.

He joined her by the rock. She did not look up. He began talking.

There were twenty to thirty people about. None observed them. Naturally they were aware of themselves, their status, but none studied. No one to question their cachet as a couple. Or whether they were friends or family. None to discern the age gap. While subtle from a distance, it was evident in his smile lines and a fading of saturation at the temples. Fourteen years apart.

He spoke quietly, foot on rock. One hand on his propped thigh. The other hand paraded through the air for verbal reinforcement.

The astute onlooker would have witnessed her tears, though without sound, nor a mere tremble of muscle. He ceased his soliloquy. Waited for a response. Expected it. Yet her head remained lowered, a picture of resignation. Then something else. A flash. A hardening. An acceptance?

IV

She was over there, crawling across a heap of cardboard and wine and discarded chairs. In an alleyway. Trying to get home. Each obstacle bypassed presented a new one in its place. It was exhausting. Debilitating. Endless.

Then she was back. Here. Arms encircling her. Thighs into the back of her legs. Naked. Bed. Spooning. It's morning. She smiles. Remembering. She pulls his hand into her chest. He mistakes it for arousal. His palm encompasses her breast. She knows he has misinterpreted but doesn't mind. Rolls back. He rises. Cups her face. Kisses her sparsely. It's the best wake up she can recall. It's only the second time's she's slept with a boy. Well, second boy. Except he is not a boy.

He's sliding over her. His kiss more determined. His tongue pressing. She's getting used to the idea, though at a pace far behind his. His knees prise her legs open. He's searching. And finding. It's like last night never ended.

Afterwards, they shower together. It's a first for her. She acts natural. Doesn't want him to know how much he's taken. Yet it feels comfortable. They laugh and chuckle. He's sarcastic but not nasty. Among other things. Emotions as sharp as the new experiences. He soaps her. He knows her body. Very well. In a short space of time. Yet it's all so fresh. Edgy. She wants to wash his body too. He's not especially muscular. Or hot. Handsome perhaps. Funny too. He knows what to say to her. And how to make her feel loved. This is so much more than her ex-boyfriend. More genuine than anything prior. Others were mere flirtations in comparison. Childlike infatuations. Her ex was obsessed, as though she were a purchased pet. Whereas He validated her. Complemented her. But allowed her space. Respected her individuality. Her personhood. Like a real woman. Yet…there was just that one thing. That age thing.

They dressed and went out for breakfast.

'Let's do something,' she said as they finished up.

'I've actually got a headache,' he laughed, genuinely weary. His resistance was not as strong as it had been a decade prior.

She rebutted his hangover as a poor excuse.

Wanting to keep pace, he made a plan. He'd been to the waterfall before. A short drive. Refresh with cold, creek water. Replenish. Restock. There'd always be afterwards. Sweet afterwards.

III

The motel was four-star, which wasn't saying much by regional standards. Clean. Serviceable. Nothing special. For him. For her, it was intimidating. Imbued with expectation. Of sex. She was nervous. Yet excited. She wanted to be there. To be with him.

He sprang onto the bed and said, 'I want this side.'

She shrugged with a 'whatever'.

He had hoped for more. A laugh. A joke. A roll around on the bed. He could tell she was apprehensive. He had to calm her. He suggested they go out for a drink. An early dinner.

The rest of the night appeared in his mind's eye, solidified before it took place. More drinks. Takeaway booze. Oil for seduction.

They walked. The town was small. Coastal. Strong breeze. Aroma of ocean. He led her down the grass to the jetty. He took her hand. They watched the fisherman go about their trade. Buckets of water. Tackle box. Grubby hair. No conversation.

He led her back to the main road. To the pub. They drank. He talked. She listened. And loosened. They ordered dinner. Laughed. Ate, drank and eyed the locals amongst the blow-ins. Being attractive and young, she received non-furtive looks from the pool players. He was all too aware. Time to slink his prize away. He bought takeaway alcohol and they hurried home. Heady with drink and the thrill of the company, they fell on each other with urgent pawing. Clothes were discarded. Hands to eager flesh. He felt younger than he had for a long time, perhaps even more than when he was actually young. They slid their naked bodies together but at opposing ends, both eager to please. And be pleased.

From there, all inhibitions and long-restrained behaviours were abandoned. They could indulge, finally, without thought to others, without the concern of age, without the worry of pleasing peers, of hiding from others, of fitting into the ideals of society. They were invisible. It allowed their emotions to take a natural path to the high winds. Before the night was over, the word love had been said six times. Four to two.

II

He lay back on her bed, feet just off the floor. She unbuttoned his pants. He was erect. She smiled. He was in awe. His heart thrashed. There was much risk. The house was empty. Her parents at work. He felt like he was reliving a non-existent teenage dream. She was slow, yet not without skill. The entire notion of it was so incredulous that he had to ask her to stop, lest the moment be concluded. He rolled her onto her back. There would be no penetration. He hadn't brought protection. He honestly hadn't anticipated this level of intensity. He had hoped for more kissing, for certain. Had expected as much after all their flirting over the three days, but he did not expect her to lead him to the bedroom as she had.

She moaned and writhed and bucked. Inside he was steaming. Was this her first time at receiving oral? She was too enthusiastic to be faking it. Attempting to keep pace, his neck became stiff. Almost to the point of cramping. He was forced to stop. She pulled him on top of her. Expectation seized him. There was a moment. A hot flush. Tempting. He rolled to one side with great regret. He explained why he could not. She accepted this and was not offended. Without hesitation, she went down on him again. Soon, very soon, it was all over. They cuddled. Secure. Still. There was a sweet silence for a time as the wind rattled the old window. On the porch the chimes played spasmodically.

She spoke, more of a whisper. 'Do you like me?'

'God yes. Very much. You're a cool chick.' He regretted the last words.

'Cool girl, you mean.'

'Spoken like a true feminist. Yes. Young woman.'

'I don't feel like a woman really. I don't think.'

'I'm not so sure about that. You're very mature. You're smart. Easy to talk to.'

'But you like me? Like that?'

'Of course. You're awesome. I mean, it's complicated. You know. Many things.'

She said nothing, which said a lot.

He kept talking and managed to keep her at bay. Soon he was laughing. Something he was adept at. His forte. They began fooling about. Like teenagers. Though it felt a little false to her, as though he believed it was what she wanted, or how she would like to behave, simply due to her age. It didn't sit right. She didn't respond enthusiastically. Hands remained limp.

Vulnerability engulfed him. Perhaps it was her lack of response which made him take a mental step back. A parent might return, or a neighbour spy them. It was without evidence yet he wanted out of the house.

'Let's get coffee. My shout.'

She seemed at ease with that.

He took her several suburbs away, further than was necessary, though at the time it felt necessary.

Following that afternoon, he did not see her for two weeks. He couldn't. He was fraught with worry and guilt, yet he could not stop thinking about her. Their texting was incessant. He was worried it would lead to them being caught. He was thorough in his discretion but could not hope for the same from a teenager, no matter how clever. What a crazy situation. Yet he hadn't felt so thrilled by the notion of a woman, a girl, for a long time. Not since he was nineteen when he was infatuated with a trainee nurse. She had pulled the earth from under him. How he had tumbled. And bled. Battered. In many ways, still bruised.

He had to do something. Change tack. More access. Freedom to breathe. A trip away. A couple of days. Nights. Bed. Her body. Her strong, flawless body. Her pool-like eyes. The buoyancy of her lips. Her slender fingers upon his face. It was more fevered than devastating hunger. A beautiful disease. To hell with convention. She was the night sky emblazoned with terrific light. How to get her away? It would take some arranging. She would have to ask her parents, wouldn't she? They were quite naive. They had no idea that their eighteen-year-old was sexually active. She was still at school and had pet guinea pigs. They knew he and she were friends, had developed a rapport over time, almost two years now, but for him to ask the parents straight out? No. That was his guilt talking. Trying to do the right thing while not. She would have to devise her own plan. She could. And would. She'd been getting away with parties and the like for years. Including a long-standing sexual relationship with a boy. The silliness of her early involvements was behind her now. She was ready for something authentic. Adult. From the exchanges they'd had, she thought of little else.

I

His friend Darren explained the rear garden's landscaping future and how far along, the plans. He nodded, fabricating interest, throwing in a couple of questions. Was Darren's final plan to sell? No, but it would increase the value of the property and who knew what lay around the corner.

They went inside, talking about their shared knowledge of electronics, specifically the current state of the industry. They had worked together in the past. They were eleven years apart and had formed a good connection, though not a particularly close one. They continued to chat while sitting down in the lounge room to watch a live football game. Darren's wife joined them, as a matter of politeness, then left to undertake some apparent work on the computer. More than likely gasbagging, jibed Darren.

They had a beer. Then another. As the game entered its final stages, Darren's stepdaughter cruised into the room. She'd been out with friends. She updated the pair on her activities of the day and the status of certain relationships.

The younger man also joined in the discussion, adding sardonic, comical remarks, prodding the teenager. How she had changed since he had met her. She gave as good as she got. He realised that it wasn't simply her physique that had altered. Perhaps being an only child provided some form of extra independence and strength of mind. She was doing very well in her final year and had plans for some sort of environmental degree. He chided that she would soon be able to produce a mean worm farm. She plopped next to him, elbowing him in the arm with considerable force. He said it hurt, which it did. Darren softly reprimanded her but she and the object of her chiding were grinning. Both were teetering on the edge of amorous dabbling. The banter continued.

Darren turned his attention to the final outcome of the game.

The two kept chatting. He was aware of a slight sensation on his thigh, like a twitch. Her hand on the leather couch between them. Her finger, tracing an inch or two back and forth. Her expression and demeanour gave nothing away. Her hand, hidden from view of her stepfather.

This was a deliberate act. What to do about it? He knew what he should do. Should. But the excitement of such minutiae was incredibly potent. It was his leg, so it didn't hurt to place his hand on it. He does so, while talking tacitly. The words carry the honesty. He's aware of how legitimate this conversation is. Instinctive. One understands by a certain age whether a conversation takes on its own life, or is pushed into existence, flapping uselessly to take flight. This was as smooth as pancake goo.

He slid his hand ever so slowly down, silent centimetres. She at the centre of a spiralling outwards galaxy. Her finger branched forth and hooked around his pinky. He drew it closer and crunched it gently. He yearned to take it further. Too much to risk. He could barely maintain a level voice. His chest yearned for more oxygen to feed his sprinting heart. It was more than the thrill of the forbidden. There was more intimacy in the pairing of fingers than he had known for years.

In several minutes, the football game was over. Darren refocused.

She detached and excused herself from the room, without gazing back, as he had desperately hoped for, to reaffirm that the tender moment was not the machinations of a teenage game, but a bona fide affection.

Was this simply a youthful flurry? An experimentation? He couldn't pursue this. It wasn't right. So why did it feel so wholly?

The next day, he would receive a text from her. She had surreptitiously garnered his number from her stepfather's phone. Just like that.

As evening came, he drove home. He found his partner of four years preparing dinner over a glass of white. She loved to cook. It had become part of the daily routine between them. Like conversation. And TV. And the bedtime ritual.

Just before sleep they had sex. Unusually, he finished in haste.

I Cook the Sausages

There's a man walking past my house. I never seen him before. Where you from, I say. He say South Korea. Stupid man. I meant where from round here. He keeps walking. Thinks I'm crazy. I'm not. Just friendly. No one's friendly. Except the man across the street. I forget his name. He's not there today. You know how? His car's gone. Yep. It's a nice day today. I like the sunny days. I'm not lazy. My wife say, You're too lazy.

No, I said. I just get tired. She doesn't listen. She's making lunch. I do the sausages. I still do good sausages. My daughter cooks her steak. She says I can't do steak her way. I can do my own steak but I just like sausages. Now. Before, I liked the steak. Hmm. I wish she will hurry up. I want the sausages now.

Hey, I remember something. My daughter. When's Sandy coming? I yell that. My voice is loud. I like my voice. My wife doesn't speak back. She should answer.

I'm outside. There's a car. I know it. It's white. Like Sandy's car. It stops. Just there. Hey! It's Sandy. She gets out. That's my daughter. She's beautiful.

Hi, Dad.

Hi, daughter. You're beautiful. I put my arms out and she falls on me. She smells real good. My daughter smell. Even if she was pretending, I could smell her.

I think she said some words but I'm talking about the cricket. I like to watch it. On the TV. My wife says I didn't use to like it. I don't remember. I like it now.

We walk inside. She says I'm squishing her hand. I didn't know. Ha ha. That's funny. I tell my wife. I squished her hand. She hugs my daughter. They talk at each other. They really talk. I don't really listen.

They talk too fast. I just like to look. At my daughter. I see my wife all the time. Every time? All the time. See? I can think properly sometimes.

My daughter comes over. She say, You're smiling.

I have to feel my face. Yes. I am.

She rubs my tummy. Says, It's big, Dad. It's getting bigger.

I say yes. It's big. It's like a big bread. Do we have bread?

Yes, says my wife.

I like to cut the big bread. I like the big piece.

My wife says, You should start cooking.

The bread?

No. The sausages.

Good. I don't like to cook the bread. I go outside. The back.

My daughter is with me. She says, How are you?

I say, I'm right here.

She says, That's good. Of course you are, Dad.

She's smiling but she is sad. That is my daughter. I know she is sad. She rubs her face.

I say, You are sad.

She shakes her head. She pats my arm like a dog.

I'm not a dog. I say that.

She laughs. I smile. She has the steak. I have to turn the barbecue on. She wants to do it. But is my job.

I say, I do it.

Okay, Dad.

I turn the dial thing and… Click Click Click Phoosh! There. Easy. See?

That's good, Dad.

She has the bottle of yellow stuff. The liquid to cook.

You do that stuff. I cook the sausages. Where are the sausages? I yell that out, two times.

Then my wife bring the sausages. This is my job. My daughter. She looks fat. I tell her.

She smiles. Rubs my arm. She says, Don't you remember? I'm pregnant.

You mean like a baby?

She say, Yes.

I say, You had the sex.

She laughs and says, Don't worry.

Who was the man? I don't like him. I might kill him.

She says, I'm married. Don't you remember?

I say, Was it Before?

Yes.

I don't remember too much Before.

She says, I know.

I say, Where's the married man who gave you the sex?

She says, 'You attacked him last time. Don't worry. He forgives you.

I don't remember.

She rubs my arm again. I look at my arm. I think she's trying to rub something off.

My wife comes out behind me. The dog barks. Not my dog. My dog is good. The little dog at the back, over the fence.

Shut up! Mutt dog! I hate that dog. It should be dead.

Sssh, Dad.

Bloody dog with the wogs! I yell that out.

Dad. Ssh. Stop it. That's racist.

I say, It's not a racing dog. A bloody stupid dog.

She keeps talking but the dog barks all the time and I want to talk to my daughter with the nice quiet and sunny day. Bloody wog dog too loud for our talking. I go down the step and pick up my dog's ball and throw it hard. Hits the fence. I want to kill the dog!

My wife says, You need to eat so you can take your pills.

I don't want the pills. They make me fall asleep and I can't watch cricket.

She says, You know you have to.

No!

My daughter has the tears.

I say, Look. You make my daughter sad!

My wife say, It's not your fault, but you need to take the pills because you could hurt yourself. Or others.

She always say that. But now I am mad. I got the Really Bads. I go and grab the rake.

My wife says, What are you doing?

I say I have to make the dog shut up. I go out the gate but something sticking at my elbow. Maybe a branch. I swish it off.

My wife is making with the crying and yelling. Really Bad. Right behind me.

I turn around. I don't know how she got there. She has her hands on her face. My daughter is with her. She looks at me with bad thoughts. My daughter. She doesn't like me.

Why don't you like me now?

She say, Coz you hit Mum.

I didn't.

Yes, you did, Dad! Jesus Christ!

I remember the branch. Was that my wife? Did I hit her? Like an accident.

My daughter says, Yes. Oh God.

Then I yell really loud and I run out my house and along the street. I can't run too fast now. That's cause of the hit on my head. It made me slow. And fat. I got the tummy. I can't remember when. I forget things. Sometimes people get angry at me. Or sad. Like now. I don't like it.

Not your fault.

But you must take the pills.

I want to remember Before. Everyone telling me I was better Before. When I was the teacher. I don't remember. I'm running down the street now. There's a metal thing in the road. The sign. It says keep left. I can still read. It thinks I'm stupid. I hit it with the rake. It makes a big sound. I hit it again. I like the sound. I want to break it. I hit it again. And then another. I got the Really Bads.

There's a car. It's stopped. People are looking at me. I yell. They should go away. Bloody dickheads. I go to the sign and hit it really hard. I'm still strong and not stupid. Not crazy. I just don't like things. Keep left. You keep the left. Fuck. I got the Bads. The Really Bads. I don't remember why. I hit the sign and the rake falls in half. I drop it on the ground. Look. One stick and one little rake. It looks funny.

Brrooooowwwwhhh.

That noise, I know it. I look up. It's the plane. Far up. The big jet. Near the cloud there. I was in one. Plane. Not cloud. Stupid. It was Before. I went somewhere. Far away. I was there for a long time. Someone wanted some money. He had metal in his hand. He got angry. Not in the plane. Somewhere else. But I don't remember. I forget things too much.

I'm in the road. That's funny. But I don't feel happy. Why am I here again?

Ah! That's my daughter. She's coming at me. In the street. She is beautiful. I should go talk to her. I have to tell her. I think she got fat.

Don't miss out! It's the last great ice shelf!

Dr Bale's two children watch the Seafarer *Cutting Edge* recede behind them as the solar chopper glides over the sleeted Southern waters. Destination: the isolated land mass that is Antarctica. Their father observes the lapping of icy grey crests but his mind is on the hotel's debut. The first true test. Being the prime investor, the glory will be all his. He's been meticulous with research and development. There's no doubting his impending success. Naturally.

He designs his entrances with a touch of showmanship and selects the final transport of the day to make the journey across the frozen landscape. Nine-year-old Ramin and eleven-year-old Jemima are in awe of the coastal mountains, though for him, the hotel's position is purely economic. No one wants a view of vague pale topography. Might as well look at a painted wall. And for a brief time, he considered it. The tourists might come, in part, to see the diminishing ice shelf, but only a fool would build on it. The entire venture was extremely expensive as it was, but a few donations in the right places can drill many an ice bore.

The other investors, representatives, management and their offspring make up the remainder of this first weekend of guests. The official opening will be the following Friday with affluent members of the public, the necessary media hoopla and some very attractive, over-excited visitors. Must have beautiful faces up front for the cameras. One couple are actually paid actors. Bale was relieved that the debacle over the hotel's name had finally been put to rest. His hand-picked project team had delivered a fiasco: Precipitation Point, Hotel Ice Break, the unimaginative South Pole Oasis, the barely pronounceable Gondwanaland Wigwam and the worst of all, the Frigid Haven, which sounded more like a Scandinavian brothel. In the end, an IT nerd presented Terra Australis Incognita. There was a meaning behind it, something to do with the early explorers. Bale didn't know or care. It possessed that exotic flavour. He took it for his own. And why not? He's the one fronting the bill.

In sight of Shackleton Range, Bale asserts into his headset, 'Circle round.'

The mountains were seemingly designed just for them. He had been to the hotel many times of course. He was there when the generators were ground into being. What an orgasmic moment that was. As is this dioramic perusal. It isn't as though he wants to value the moment with his two children. It never crosses his mind. It is simply masturbatory in context. He's a dedicated enthusiast for 'self-service', and always has been. In part because no one else can live up to his expectations. And yet, he demands that he first earns the privilege and thus creates the recipe for his success. His affliction with this particular pleasure once bothered his wife, but she ceased complaining after their children were born. He refused to hire a nanny. Not for his blood. For the most part, his wife was maternally too preoccupied to lament her scant sex life. As far as he was concerned, she was fulfilling her purpose and he severed his counterfeit devotion to her. Another objective reached.

An hour later they are in the Presidential Suite.

'Open,' Ramin says.

The windows become translucent, allowing the white to slice in.

'Jesus!' says Dr Bale.

'Sorry Father. Dim.' The glass darkens.

His sister Jemima says, 'You're the dim one, Ramin.'

Ramin stares evil. 'Watch it! Or you'll be skating across thin ice. Ha ha! Get it?'

'You two control yourselves. Admire the view. It bloody well cost me enough.'

Ramin analyses the spotty distance. 'What's that? Is that the penguins?'

Bale drops an ice cube into his Scotch and ambles over. 'Damn well better be.'

Jemima says, 'Can we go out and see them?'

'That's tomorrow's agenda.'

'Where's the rest of them?' Ramin asks.

Bale scrutinises. 'That's the lot.'

'But Daddy, you said there'd be heaps of them!'

Bale places a firm hard on the boy's shoulder. 'They were here when we first arrived. It's not my fault if they got cold feet.'

'Was that…a joke, Father?'

Jemima looks faint. 'So where's the rest?'

'Do you have to ask so many questions, Jemima? Annoying girl. Infractions, all right? Fractals. Something like that. Dirty water. Does it matter? It wasn't like this in the planning stages. Don't worry about that. Certain people have paid the price.'

Ramin says, 'They'll be getting jobs in waste purging, Father?'

Bale sniffs his Scotch. 'They won't be getting any jobs.'

'Yeah, Jem germ. You're so stupid.'

'Father!' she complains.

'Are you two always like this? I'm sure your mother is sick on purpose.' He downs the Scotch while the two youngsters homicidally glare at each other.

'Make me another scotch, Ramin. Then prepare for dinner.'

'Father, is this going to be another dull business meeting?' Jemima says, hand on hip.

'This is important. People look to me for guidance.'

'Yep, it's boring,' Ramin groans.

'It's time you two began acting like Bales. The world would be in utter chaos without people like us. As I've explained, there are two types. Those who lead and those who follow.'

Ramin hands his father the Scotch. 'It's okay, Father. I'll show them. If Jem germ can't.'

She shoots her brother a death pout.

'God help me,' Bale says. 'Listen, you brats, if you behave, I may swing an early trip on *The Submerger*.' He had planned it already.

The children look to each other with creeping smiles.

'Tonight?'

'Don't be idiotic. Tomorrow, depending on your performance.'

'Maximum attitude, Father,' Jemima says.

'No, idjit,' says Ramin. 'It's maximum aptitude!'

'That's correct, Ramin. Jemima, no need to brown-nose. A Bale never capitulates, even when all is lost. Understand?' He would have to explain the intricacies of brown-nosing when they were older. Nothing wrong with getting a little shit on your face, as long as someone else wipes it off.

Less than ninety minutes later, while the one hundred and sixty guests eat, Bale makes his speech. It appears unrehearsed, but that's the point. A brief dot-point scan and four Scotches are all he needs. And perhaps a taste of that Asian waitress flitting amongst the front tables. He detects the awe on her face. Naturally.

After the applause fades, he makes his way to the kitchen. The staff are surprised to see him. They are clearly unnerved. The head waiter rushes over. Bale demands a Scotch. The waiter motions to a female kitchen hand. Bale studies her as she locates the bottle and pours him a drink. She's not up to his benchmark.

When the glass is in his hand, Bale takes the waiter aside. He makes enquiries about the Asian waitress he had observed. Coincidentally, just as the two men converse, she enters. She is attractive, strong-featured and young. With certain poise, it seems she could be destined for better things. Right now, she is without power and, therefore, easily manipulated. The waiter obediently approaches her. The girl does not appear enthusiastic, even after the waiter presents her with the roll of credit vouchers Bale had slipped him. She looks up. Bale applies his Bond look. Uncertainty is the only thing that makes life interesting, provided he gets his way in the end. And that's a certainty.

Later when his children are asleep, Bale makes his way down to the kitchen, where the remaining staff members are cleaning up.

'You can leave now.'

'Oh hello, sir. We just have one more...'

'Leave now or leave permanently.'

In a flash, he is alone, but not for long. Just as he pours fresh but inferior kitchen Scotch, she appears, loitering coyly at the far end of the tiled workspace like a gunslinger. She might be Chinese but he can't be certain. Her background is irrelevant. It's her body he wants. There's a provocative manner about her. Yet she seems untouched. Just how he likes them. Her youth is scintillating. Or perhaps it's the Scotch beginning to claim him. He knows he's had too many but pours another. Neat. No ice. A real man. He raises his glass to her in offering.

She declines.

He downs half of it. He motions for her to come closer.

She remains stationary. Not a tease. Insubordinate.

'Do you like working here?'

Bewilderment then consternation moves across her face like a shadow. Did she detect a threat?

'It's a genuine question,' he says. 'I saw how efficiently you were working and I thought, there goes someone who enjoys her job.'

Her eyes narrow.

'I'm not trying to patronise you. I'm sure you actually detest it, but the method is in deceiving yourself. I can relate to that. Goes for anything. Business, relationships, marriage.'

'I like this place. The Antarctic, I mean.'

He nods. 'I knew there was something you were passionate about.'

'I studied Ice Dissipation at university.'

'You're not one of those enviro types, are you?' His smirk does not hide his contempt.

'I never completed my degree. I just want to travel, you know?'

'We've had infiltrators here before, you see. They were dealt with harshly. I wouldn't recommend it.' The recipe for his success.

She seems to ignore his remark. 'I like to meet different people. And experience new things. Same as everybody else.'

He sups his Scotch. 'I'm arranging a trip for my children tomorrow. On the *Submerger*.'

'Yes?' She steps forward. 'We must work for six months before we get to go. I suppose you knew that already.'

'I didn't, but I do now. I'll look into it.' Fabrication is necessary in business. Why would he waste a costly enterprise on staff? 'Come closer. It's awkward having a conversation over this distance. You're very intuitive. That's why I didn't patronise you.'

She looks down. 'I don't want to jeopardise my position here.'

'Don't fret, sweetheart. I'm not going to attempt to have sex with you. What was going through your mind? I've got children.' He smiles and drains the Scotch.

'Oh, of course.' She is somewhat embarrassed and shuffles forward. 'Sorry.'

He puts the glass down. 'I just want you to stand there a minute. Come closer.'

She obeys. 'Um, okay. Is this a game of some kind?'

'Everything's a game. Most people are too stupid to realise it. They bunker down on their pointless principles and pretend it has some higher meaning.' He reaches out and grasps her shoulder. 'Don't move.' He unzips his fly and reaches in.

She flinches but his fingers dig into her sinews.

'I'm not going to touch you beyond this. I will arrange for you to be on the *Submerger* tomorrow. In addition to that and more importantly, you can keep your job, even if you are a fucking enviro. But if you move, I will have you fired. If you complain, I'll have you up on charges as an infiltrator. You must watch. Do not turn away.' He begins masturbating.

She can scarcely comprehend what's happening, let alone analyse a way out without compromising herself. Maybe he knows.

'I come from a long line of Bales. We've always been pioneers. This is the last ice shelf and I have brought it to the world. Let them have one last look. As long as they pay for the privilege. And if it disappears, which it probably will, I'll create other opportunities.' His tone becomes more erratic. 'Hell, I'll manufacture the fucking ice and claim it as genuine.'

She feels sick but also rage. It's taking all of her preparation to hold it together. They hadn't told her that it would be this difficult. Focus on the objective. You don't matter.

'I'll show you the way, sweetheart,' he says panting. 'I'll show you. I will…' He ejaculates onto the tiled floor and her black shoes.

Naturally.

To reach the *Submerger* they must take a short shuttle trip from the hotel. An infrared turnstile identifies each person. The excitement of those present, the investors, management and their children drowns out the safety instructions. Soon they are gliding across the grey landscape, patches of rock already free of the dirty white ice, the temperature not what it was.

Dr Bale yawns, his second caffeine having eluded him. He turns to one of the middle management sycophants grinning next to him and says, 'Environmental concerns, blah blah. Let's just get this over with.'

The man laughs, a tad too eagerly.

Ramin gives his father a stern look. 'Maybe you wouldn't be so tired, Father, if you didn't drink so much Scotch.'

'Fertile imagination, these kids.' Bale resists the urge to smack his son across the face. 'Prefer to go back, Ramin? I can arrange it.'

Jemima grins. 'Please do, Father.'

Ramin turns in time to see the shuttle enter the metal dome. They slide to a halt and exit in accordance with status. Bales first. The shuttle empties behind them. Down metal stairs to a platform, air crisp, breath showing. They receive more instructions, the hurried version for the executives. A panel slides open and behold, the tall spherical *Submerger*, shaped like a perfect pearl tear drop. The children are wide-eyed with marvel. Bale is droopy, thinking only of coffee. And perhaps an afternoon nap. Alert enough to notice, however, that the waitress is a no-show. He will have to monitor her. Any hint of trouble and she will suddenly commit an unforgivable employee error.

The recipe for his success.

They file into the transport. The floor and part of the curved walls are made of thick transparent perspex, in order to maximise viewing pleasure. At the moment, though, all they can see is the circular metal grille below, the only thing between them and the aqueous chasm. The guide ensures that all are seated and strapped in tight around the periphery. After securing the hatch and more instructions, they are ready.

Bale senses claustrophobia swarming in. It's all about control. He does not like situations without it. Are you scared? The Bales are not claustrophobic! His father taught him that example. Hours in a storage box. Part of the tests.

Weakness is for peasants!

I am not… I am not…

Bale fights it back the only way he can. The inner voice calming his child. The hangover has allowed his nemesis to creep in. Damn cheap commoner's Scotch.

The guide is the last to strap in.

The grate clanks, yawning.

The children become quiet. Excited yet edgy.

The submersible groans.

The dark freezing water is revealed. Ominous. Not yet ready to reveal its secrets.

Anxiety settles in, tendrils reaching out.

To everyone that is, except Bale. He has won the battle over his panic. For now.

The thick steel cable unwinds, lowering the *Submerger* stealthily, almost like a spermatozoa making its way into the canal.

Gloom encompasses, an immediate night.

The open grate diminishes overhead, like a train receding from the tunnel mouth.

Pitch, nightmarish black.

Jemima grips her father's forearm. He doesn't reassure her. She needs toughening, like the other scaredy-cats around them, some sniffling in fear. Still, he would have to demand that adequate lighting is present in this early stage. The attempt at a mysterious atmosphere is too frightening for children.

Floodlights shimmer outwards.

Everyone murmurs, more from relief, until the beauty of the spectacle seeps through their diminishing dread. The illumination reveals a colossal valley of ice; a terrifying, but stunning unknown universe. More impressive than any penguin visit.

Bale knew this of course. The penguins would always be a let-down. Declining habitat and so on. It doesn't matter. As long as the tourists come. The *Submerger* would satiate any apparent qualms. Give them a circus ride and the little people are content.

The waters are thick with slush, drifting particles.

Tiny amoebas investigate, then ignore.

A child presses against the limpid wall, astounded.

'Beautiful,' whispers Ramin.

Bale glowers. The boy is a trifle soft, perhaps gay, but there is still time.

There is a faraway thud, as though coming from the surface. It did not come from the docking station. Or did it? Somewhere close. An unnatural sound. Not of nature. A giant net of ripples tracks toward them. It hits the *Submerger*, tilting it violently, a shifting metallic groan followed by a hush of terrified souls.

'Is this part of the ride?' Jemima asks.

deeBRRRRUWrrrr rr r

Another muffled detonation. Much closer this time. That's what it is, isn't it? A fucking explosion. Bale seethes. Some incompetent arsehole's going to pay.

Outside, half of the world is closing in. The glacier is moving.

'What the hell's happening?' Bale spits at the guide. 'Why are we moving towards the ice?'

The guide rises to his feet. 'We're not.'

They are being severely buffeted.

Not without difficulty, he makes it to the controls. 'Oh, God.'

Detecting his mood, the occupants tense. The children are crying. Some shriek. Adults attempt to calm them, others are demanding answers and solutions, but there's no one who can soothe their terror.

They can see the grate overhead, linked by the cable, their umbilical cord, but the station seems so far away.

Falling frozen pebbles turn to boulders. They pound the transparent roof.

Bale flaps. 'Get us back right now, you arsehole!'

The glacier bears down hard against their embryo, earth quaking.

The guide is thrown off his feet and smacks his skull on the floor. Everyone is too preoccupied to care.

'Father?' Jemima tugs on his arm, the urge for reassurance in her eyes.

Bale knows what's going to happen. It's only seconds away. He unleashes his belt and heads for the controls. The guide is on the floor, not moving. Inept fool.

Bale waves across the controls. The visual display reveals they are already retracting, as fast as possible by the looks of it. He looks up to confirm, but the grate is no longer visible. A skyscraper of ice has blocked them in.

'Damn it. How do I access communications on this thing?'

The tips of the glaciers converge. Ice pounds against ice, sandwiching the cable. Metal shreds. Unable to stand the enormous forces at play, the cable snaps.

Bale is hurled to the floor.

All power dies and blackness consumes them. Without heating, the cold already begins to permeate the shell. They are left with the grumbling sounds of Mother Nature's frozen vigour.

The *Submerger* oscillates, a mere drop in a torrent of fever sweat.

Children howl. Adults scream but their sounds are confined by the embryonic fluid. He hears Jemima crying but soon she is relegated to the outside world as he returns to his father's storage box.

Lying on the cold hard plastic in the dark, trembling with

claustrophobia, Bale shrinks into a foetal position. His hand finds its way between his legs. For once, he is limp. There is no recipe for failure.

The *Submerger* is nothing now but a fluttering stamp in a cock-eyed whirlpool. It plunges beneath the dual glaciers as the bulk of the ice comes together with tremendous energy, a tearing heavenly crash.

The down current from the collision seizes them, mere sediment in an eddy. They corkscrew down and down, further into the uncharted virgin womb.

Naturally.

Creatures of Habitual

You never quite know when and how much your life will change, no matter how much it's dominated by routine.

As she read the front page of the local Shell Harbour paper, she had to smile. Her partying days were well and truly over and wasn't that a blessing. The article in question was about two paramedics who had been attacked while on the job. They were attending to an assault victim in the town centre late on Saturday night when they themselves were set upon. She shouldn't really smile. It was a terrible situation and a sad reflection of where many of today's juveniles were at.

Youth had never respected authority and the commentators were fooling themselves thinking that they had. There did seem to be an increase in alcohol-related violence. No one thought anything of a group setting upon one person or attacking someone with a glass or bottle. In her day, you would be a labelled a coward for such an act. A fight was one against one or a gang against another gang.

The article reminded her of teenage days of trouble, tears, tantrums, confusion and heartbreak. Oh yes, plenty of heartache. An ocean of pain, the emotions as swirling and unpredictable as the currents. She was glad that it was all behind her. Today her life was the polar opposite. She was sixty-three and had become the person she swore she'd never be, just like her mother. If anything, her life was even more structured.

Her days went like this. She rose at 6.47 after one hit on the snooze button. She let the cat out, His Majesty Fernando, and made breakfast. She ate it at precisely 7.30. She washed the dishes and had a shower. She put on her make-up and left the house at 8.40 and not a minute later. She walked to the corner store and bought the paper. She could have it delivered but she likes the walk and the nice man who runs the store, Mr Chan. While not overly chatty, he is polite and knows her name, which in itself, warrants the journey. She walks home, lets the cat in, makes a pot of tea, enough for two cups and reads the paper. At 9.45, she begins her housework regime, which takes precisely one hour. She dusts, vacuums (those cat hairs), makes her bed and a quick once over of the bathroom (it's already spotless).

Monday the bins go out. Tuesday she returns the weekly DVDs and rents a new batch (always three). Wednesday is lottery day. Thursday is lunch with the girls at the quaint little café near the mall (the RSL is for drunks and gamblers) followed by a library visit. Friday is lawn bowls. If possible, depending on the weather, she will sweep the concrete paths around her house. If wet, a little polishing of the items in her cabinet, the animal figurines, souvenirs and family photographs. Though she never had children, there were many slightly faded shots of her nieces and nephews and now, some of their children.

Lunch is a simple ham and salad sandwich with a side plate of cut-up fruit (apple and banana), though in winter she makes a tomato or pumpkin soup with bread.

Somehow or other, twenty-three years before, she had stumbled upon one of the prominent afternoon soaps and had become deliciously hooked. She doesn't feel as though she must watch it, it's more like visiting old friends. The characters give her a sense of warmth, even if their behaviour is often questionable.

Following that, it's off to the local shopping district by car to buy her groceries, pay the bills and whatever else requires her attention. She comes home, feeds Fernando (the first of two meals, as he prefers to eat late), has a cup of tea and a wee slice of cake, which she makes on a Sunday, a spot of reading, a good old-fashioned mystery and then onto dinner preparation by five, dinner at six, washing up, ABC news, a change into her nightie, followed by a variety of her favourite shows, spread throughout the week. Friday and Saturday nights were

DVD nights. There were many more things, such as reading in bed for twenty minutes before sleep and others so exacting that she no longer needed to rely on the eight clocks spread throughout the house even though she scanned them meticulously. Such is habit.

Evening arrived. Friday. DVD night. Tonight's film was an Australian drama about ten years old with the usual Aussie characters and woes (why do they have to swear so much?). The stories might change, but it appeared to her as though they were all made by the same people. Perhaps they were. A comforting thought. However, it was over two hours long. She had stayed up later than usual, which was no accident, as her precise bedtime was determined by the movie's length. Live a little. Yet now she was dead-tired. There was something else. Something out of place. The cat. 'Oh no, Fernando!' He would be waiting for her at the door and probably had been for some time.

She slides open the glass door, expecting to see his little eyes staring up from the step so much so that it takes her seconds to grasp that he isn't actually there. She can make out half the yard with the light leaking from the kitchen, but the rest is in darkness. She calls out his name. He doesn't come. She figures he is probably sick of waiting for the silly woman and has wandered off somewhere. Should she leave the door open and hope that he will return? How long would that be? She decides to fetch the torch from the bottom of the pantry behind her garden shoes. She discovers that the shoes are a tad grotty and in need of a good wipe. Mess can not be tolerated.

She slides the door closed behind her and flicks the torch on. She plays the beam over the backyard. The light brings momentary respite to the gloom. Her glasses don't help. They are merely short-distance glasses. She calls out to him, treading across the perfectly cut lawn (a garden man comes every fortnight), stopping in front of the small trees and bushes which line the back fence. She swings the light over them, the shadows thick and floating. He always comes when she calls. So it is logical that he is not here. She turns and walks down the side of the house. The path leads to the gate and out onto the street. The gate is shut, which of course, means nothing. It wouldn't be the first time he's jumped the fence.

The street light beckons. It is brighter out. She should get a clear view. She pulls her nightie tight around her and opens the gate. She surveys the front yard, calling softly to Fernando. She doesn't want to scare him away nor disturb the neighbours, lest they think her odd. This is not like her at all. The torch does not reveal any clues. The surrounding houses appear quiet, save for a barking dog further up the street. She hopes that it is not barking at Fernando. He could be backed up against a fence, frozen with fear. Perhaps she should take a look. She treads slowly up the pavement, her slippers soft on the concrete. The street is still, save for the muffled sounds of televisions and bluish flickers from beyond curtains. She has to have her Fernando home. She will not be able to sleep without him.

The street is different in the dark. It's like another world. She can't remember the last time she was out at night. It's almost as though she's walking on the moon, an explorer. The Arctic Circle, without the ice. She finds it strangely invigorating but has to focus on the cat. The barking increases in intensity and ups her anxiety. As she gets closer, she realises it's merely one of those tiresome yappy mutts that would howl at a bird fluff. She walks on. It's more illuminated at the next cross street, a busier road. Perhaps he was attracted by the noise and lights. It seems an awfully busy and dangerous place for a wee cat.

As she walks, she remembers that it is Friday night, which would account for the traffic. Still, she has never seen it so busy. The streets have certainly changed over the years. She is tempted to go back home, but can't return without him. She keeps calling for Fernando.

A car slows. It's a group of young people, ogling.

A young lady yells out, 'Hey, grandma! Where's ya wand? Woo-hoo!'

Such disrespect. She is no one's grandma. She isn't even old. Perhaps she isn't young any more, but is still middle-aged, thank you very much. That's if she doesn't catch cold from being outside. What was she thinking being out this late in her nightie no less? And yet the breeze on her cheeks and the faint salt sprinkle of stars above make her feel lively. There is an energy in the air. A slight hint of adventure too. A feeling that she has not had since being young so long ago, when she was literally a different person.

She is so preoccupied looking in every shadow for him that she doesn't notice them until they are almost upon her. It's a group of young 'uns. Four male and one female and nearly all of them drinking. At first she believes it's the carload returned to target her. She stops. It's not the same kids. They are curious. They quickly surround her. They look her up and down as though she belongs to another species.

'She's pretty hot, hey!'

'Ha ha. You idiot.'

'Maybe she's lost.'

'Escaped from the old farts' home.'

'Cool. On the run, hey.'

'Hard bitch.'

'She's bananas. In pyjamas!'

They laugh, encouraging one another.

One elbows another. 'See if she's up for a shag.'

They explode in a cauldron of splutters and fall over themselves in a tirade of teenage limbs, each aiming to impress the other.

'Please. Have you seen my Fernando?'

'Your what?'

More giggling.

'Wait, she's trying to say something,' says a boy.

'My cat,' she says. 'He's lost. Have you seen him?'

Another boy says, 'She wants to know if you've seen her pussy.'

They laugh and one boy pushes another towards the sixty-three-year-old. Purely as a defensive instinct, she swings the torch. There's a coarse crack and the boy drops. Another boy chuckles. She realises it's no laughing matter. She backs away. A girl and a boy go to the injured teen, who has not moved. For a moment, they think he's kidding. But it's no joke.

'What'dya do that for?'

'You bitch!'

She takes a step back. 'I didn't mean it!'

The girl on the pavement says, 'Call an ambulance!'

Two boys walk towards their new nemesis, hate on their faces. 'Where do you think you're going?'

She holds out the torch to them, as though giving it up will undo the action. 'I'm sorry. It was a reflex.'

The young girl is speaking into her mobile phone, perhaps calling for reinforcements. In the meantime, the boys are calling her names that she has not heard for decades, apart from in films, occasionally in the street and that unfortunate time inside the butcher shop when a customer argued over the price of Italian sausages. She drops the torch.

One of them picks it up and holds it back like a cricket ball as though she is the stumps. 'I'll do it to you, old bitch!'

She pictures her house, her chair, her kitchen, her clocks, her bed. All she wants is her bed. That stupid cat, Fernando. This is his fault. 'I'm sorry. I'm so sorry.' She recalls the newspaper articles. The assaults, the vicious beatings, the lack of respect, society seemingly without rules. She knows she has no recourse. She has handed them an excuse on a platter. She will be the one in the next day's papers. Someone just like her will read about the incident and shake their head and wonder what the world is coming to. Then they'll put the paper down and have a cup of tea and simply forget. That's all she'll be, a scant few lines in the local rag. She doesn't even have children. There'll be a funeral of course, some faint dabbing beneath the eyes with a handkerchief. A wake with tea and biscuits. A missing position in the bowls team, which will be filled quickly and that will be it. Gone. As though she was nothing. All of those years sticking rigidly to her schedule will count for naught. Did her routines ever do her any good?

The two lads circle her like a pair of fasting falcons, wondering which piece of flesh to tear first.

She is rigid. There is no point crying. It's too late. It had all been a silly mistake. Just one slip-up in a vacuum-sealed life. Why hadn't she stayed home?

She hears a siren, enlarging. An ambulance?

A third boy rapidly approaches the others. 'Come on, guys. She's just an old woman. She didn't mean it. Did you?'

She shakes her head, unable to speak.

'Come on. I'll walk you home. Do you know where you live? Where's the nursing home?' He lightly takes her by the arm. 'This way, is it?'

She's not sure how to take him. She wants to believe that he has genuine intentions but nothing tonight slots into her beliefs, her experiences. What world is this?

The youngsters look to each other for guidance, but find none. They merely wait for someone to tell them what to do.

The ambulance pulls up. A young man and a woman get out, but they hesitate. They personally know the paramedic who was recently attacked. He remains in a serious condition. For all they know, it's the same group of teenagers.

'Step away from the victim,' says the woman.

The girl cradles the injured boy's head and indicates with her own that she will not obey.

The young woman points. 'We're not coming over there until you back away. The lot of you.'

The male paramedic becomes aware of the elderly woman in her flimsy nightie with a teen holding her arm forcibly, about to do or having already done God knows what disgusting thing, all in the arena of pubescent entertainment. Sick little shits. Action. Not reaction. The paramedic charges at the boy, who barely has time to speak as he is tackled to the ground with full force, almost bowling over the sixty-three-year-old. The other two boys rush in to help, fists and feet in high rotation. The female paramedic is shouting into her radio. The woman in her pyjamas rights herself and runs, yes, she actually runs, which is the first time for many years and she isn't fast but is a lot faster than she thinks possible and perhaps bowling has given her some exercise after all.

In no time, she is back in the darkened streets more familiar to her. She is astounded that no one is pursuing, instead detecting another siren, one she recognises as from a police car. She slows as she is reunited with the secure outlines of neighbours' houses. Her bosom heaves as she tries to catch up on oxygen. Soon she is at her side gate, spluttering. Her throat is dry and her temples are clobbering.

She staggers into her backyard. The back light is on. On the steps by the door sits Fernando like a celebrity, waiting but indifferent to her state. She squints as she gets closer. He licks his lips, anticipating food. That little twerp. That's all she is to him. A Walking Supermarket. A Portable Drive-through. Her throat is raw from her toil, but still she screams, 'You fucking little bastard shit of a cat!' She kicks Fernando and he scissors backwards into the glass door, bounces off, rotates in a blur and bounds screeching off into the night.

She opens the door and slides it shut hard behind her, locking it with a sense of finality. She stumbles panting to the cupboard. From the rear of the second highest shelf she seeks out a bottle of whiskey. It's been there for over a year thanks to her nephew, who insisted it be stored there, no doubt to tolerate the boredom of visiting her. Well, fuck him too.

She stays awake until the sky is blue and gets drunk as a maggot in a beer vat.

She sleeps most of the next day, neglecting her breakfast, the dishes, her shower, all of it. She also forgoes buying the paper, therefore not discovering the outcome of her ordeal in a small paragraph on page four. However, she is successful in eradicating most of her routines forever more.

Without him.

Don't Bring Me Down

The river eased up over the bridge like cling film, the road still visible beneath, but not for long. The water was a mucky brown like beef soup, fast-flowing, carrying leaves, branches and the remnants of parks, bins and the yards of those who lived within range of the overrun.

Around eight people stood at the mouth of the bridge, three of them adults. A man was telling the children not to get close as they were too young to remember the previous flood, some fourteen years gone, where a mother and her eleven-year-old son had drowned. While it hadn't rained all morning, the downpour during the night ensured that the level was still rising. He knew it not to be underestimated.

A car was coming down the slight incline towards them, a small white Mitsubishi, a lone woman inside, clearly determined to brace the crossing. The man in his thirties shook his head, his face a mess of silent outrage. He manoeuvred into her intended path. She made it clear, though going slow, that she was not stopping for a chat.

'Hey, don't do it!' he dictated with authority born of understanding, yet she rolled past, her window down, her hair big and recently attended to, perhaps that very morning.

She was in her fifties and, though he had seen her before, did not know her name. He did know that she was not around during the '99 disaster. Yet wisdom is not synonymous with experience and perhaps it wouldn't have mattered if she had been.

'Stupid woman,' he shouted, ensuring she would hear.

The other adults and children gazed in disillusionment as her wheels quickly disappeared beneath the surface. He shook his head and heard her reply, quite garishly, such as 'husband' or 'home' or something, but the dull groan of the river removed her full comment.

'She's not going to make it,' he said.

The children looked to him. One of them was his nine-year-old son. His dad knew what he was talking about.

'She might,' said another man, though much younger, who some might class as a boy, the local apprentice plumber.

The bridge was not long, but under the conditions had never seemed longer. It wasn't particularly wide, enough for a car in both directions and a footpath to one side, which was protected from the road by an iron fence.

'If it was a four-wheel drive, maybe,' the man stated. 'The river's coming up fast. The engine's too low. It's gunna stall. Any idiot can see that.'

It was a perverse festival, a controlled reality program without the cameras. On the opposing side of the bridge stood a man and his wife, long-term residents who could determine what was unfolding.

The water was relentless. The car slackened over the course of several metres. Then it quit altogether.

'What did I tell ya? Total moron.'

The young man did not like being wrong yet managed a half-smirk.

The nine-year-old was filled with pride. He never doubted that his dad was right.

The woman's hand emerged from the car window, beckoning.

'Is she royalty?' the man said.

The kids chuckled.

The younger man waved to her in mockery, 'Hi, your Highness!'

The children laughed again.

The man accentuated his groan. He turned to the other. 'You'd better help me.'

'It's her own dumb fault. Let her work it out. '

The man took his shoes off. 'Come on, we can do this but we better go now.'

There was the briefest of debates. Also concern from the man's son. The risk factor was also reinforced by the only other adult there, a woman, known to the man's family. The man knew all of this of course but the emergency services would be busy, as numerous houses and farms in the area were already engulfed. There simply wasn't time. The man felt partially responsible too. Perhaps there was also a sliver of ego that wanted his son to lay witness to a heroic deed, a tale for decades to come.

The young man reluctantly followed but was already some metres behind. It was evident that the water was still rising. It was up around their thighs. He could see the woman half-hanging out of her window, the water not far below. It signified that it was already inside her car and up to the hips of the man in front. He wondered if the bridge was sagging. He had a horrible feeling that it was about to break in two, like the *Titanic*. He looked behind him, aware of the worry in the faces staring back. This was no longer a game and never had been. He realised that he had not appreciated the severity of the situation. He was jeopardising his life for a dickhead. It might be wiser to turn back. He clocked the older man's kid. There was a mixture of excitement, the expectation of the unknown and worry in his face. The young man was committed. Besides, the town expected real men and he did not want to be labelled a pussy.

The father was close upon the car, though it was clear he had to use all his strength to remain upright. The pedestrian fence might protect them from being swept away if they were to fall but it was only chest-high and could not be relied upon for much longer.

The woman reached out to him. She wasn't crying yet was agitated and in danger of making a decision in haste. He signalled for her not to move.

At that moment, the young man swore he saw the car move sideways, just a fraction. He paused, unsure what to do, peering back again to see the woman with the children on her phone, hopefully calling the right people. Yet something was happening now, not in ten or even five minutes. When he turned back, he noticed that the car had moved again, no denying it now. This time, it wasn't stopping. The water had picked it up as though a bath toy. The woman literally dove out the window. The man bent forward to grab her, slipped and went under. He shot up again, somehow taking hold of the woman but both were swept against the car, which in turn, slammed into the fence. The wire held, for the time being, but the water pushed up and over them like a fountain. They spluttered, turning their faces from it, struggling to keep their mouths clear, not helped by the woman's hysteria.

The young man thought it best to return. He was scared. It was increasingly arduous simply to remain fixed. He was forced to lean into the water to prevent from being overcome. What the hell had he been thinking? There was nothing he could do anyway. As he turned, he saw an immense clump of river junk, the size of half a dozen people, coming directly at him. Sticks, branches and leaves had coalesced together. Instinctively, he placed his hands out in a futile gesture to the indiscriminate debris, lost his balance and went under. He felt the drag and was a part of it. He took water into his mouth, clawing desperately towards the light, just as he slammed into the fence. The forces of nature flipped him over it, slinging him into the malevolent, impervious downstream swell.

Luv u 4eva

Mark is tall, dark and handsome and only months away from leaving his teens behind. Finally! Sophie is small and blonde and much sought-after yet, despite her poise and cultivated constitution, is only fifteen (and two-thirds).

There was no hiding their coming together. The moment of their first kiss (from multiple angles) was captured and shared thanks to flashing phones illuminating the dark corner at the party. She'd been dead sober. He, not so much. He didn't learn of her actual age until days later. She had tracked him down. It took some initiative. When Sophie wanted something, she got it.

She may have been 'age-challenged' yet it was a fact that came too late for Mark. He was smitten. She looked eighteen and was undoubtedly smarter than he. And most of his mates. Probably all of them.

'I'll love you forever,' he said. Often.

'I love you too, baby,' she would reply, though a wise whisper inside knew that it wouldn't last. She had her entire life ahead of her. She would marry someone more sophisticated. Someone with more prospects than an apprentice mechanic. For now, that bad boy had a car. And he was sexier than a slicked-up soapie star. A selfie star!

They'd done their best to keep it from her parents by limiting certain connections such as Facebook (but not Instagram) and texting rather than late-night calls.

A few weeks back, in the privacy of his car at a McDonald's car park, things had become so intense that had it been winter, they could have drawn pictographs on the windows. Just like in *Titanic*.

'I can't. They'll kill me,' he said, referring to her parents and the age difference.

'I'm not talking about doing *it*,' she said. 'I just want to have some fun, okay?'

'I'm being serious. I could go to jail. I respect you too much.'

Her friends were expecting a story of passion. She slapped the seat, 'Oh, my God!'

He slipped away from her, attempting to regain his breath. It wasn't easy. 'We'll have plenty of time for fun, sweetie. I gotta do the right thing. Your parents will find out eventually. I don't want them to hate me. I'm gunna be a part of your family, you know.'

'I won't tell. I promise.'

'I know, babe. But someone else could.'

'What are you saying?'

'I dunno, babe. Just trust me, all right? This is the best way. I really want to get naked with you but shit, girl, I gotta do the right thing.'

She agreed but whined to her friends, especially Taylyn, who was the only one of her group to have actually done *it*. Taylyn also had the hots for her boyfriend's mate, Joseph. So when the opportunity arose for the four of them to get together on a Friday night (both girls said they were staying at the other's) they went for it.

Mark's car is black with shiny hubcaps. She doesn't know the make. Who cares? It's loud and fast and everyone looks at them when they drive past. They cruise the inner western streets. Occasionally they yell out at people. They laugh. The music is loud. The lights are bright and colourful. It's a great time to be young, isn't it? The world belongs to them! All four share their experiences with their network via their phones, including Mark. What's the point of being cool if you can't make your friends jealous? Lol!

They hit the drive-through bottle shop. The girls want cruisers. Mark is pressured to buy them.

Joseph buys a six-pack of cheap beer. 'I'm gunna need all six, bro.'

Mark says, 'Don't worry, mate. None for me. Don't wanna lose my licence.'

'Ah, you can have one, bro.'

He turns to Sophie. 'Nah. Gotta do the right thing by my girl.'

'Cringey,' she says.

He runs his hand through her blonde locks. Her eyes shimmer back at him. He's got it good. If only she were a bit older.

With an hour, Taylyn and Joseph are getting it on in the back. Sophie keeps looking back at them. She'd take a photo of the action if she wasn't so annoyed. Or jealous. Or something. Sophie is supposed to be the leader of their group at school, yet Taylyn is going to be the one with the story. Mark hasn't lifted a finger! Why do they have to keep driving round and round? Isn't she hot enough? Is he gay or what? She stares at him with accusatory eyes.

'What's up, babe?'

She shakes her head and looks out at the cars they pass. She opts to flick through her news feed.

Mark doesn't understand her change in mood. What's wrong with girls? So confusing. He can't talk to Joseph. Lucky dude has his hands full. He opts to text a friend. Maybe he can work out Sophie's problem. He needs someone onside. *Hey, bro. Check it. Soph givin me dirtys.*

His car drifts into the next lane.

I don't get girls…

They clip the back of a ute, which spins to the left. Mark ploughs into the ute. The cars are briefly entwined in a design-less ballet until Mark's car slaps the gutter, sending them up into the air and smashing into an iron fence. The crushed metal plunges to the pavement, passenger side down.

The ute is hit by one other car and, remarkably, other cars manage to brake in time. Debris decorates the road like toddler's art.

Somehow, no one is killed, other than Sophie, whose section of the vehicle received the force of the impact, her blonde locks matted with clumps of blood and bone. The left side of her skull is dinted like plasticine. The couple in back will eventually recover, though will never be the same. Yet it's Mark who is almost injury-free, left with the memory of his true love and decades to ponder the true meaning of 'doing the right thing'.

Officer Material

I stomp through the ooze, with barely enough energy to continue. I'm on second point. My buddy Haken is behind me to the right.

Be careful. They mould you into what they want. They'll tell you anything, but not the real thing. Only the promise of adventure and glory. All for the honour of serving humanity.

I was like a mouse wandering into a pack of feral cats. A misguided sacrifice. No wonder they kept the truth from us.

The ground is sodden by the rain. Heavy condensation hangs perpetually in the air. It's so thick you can almost swipe aside the beads. It's constantly dripping into your eyes but we are so dirty that if you touch your face, it risks infection. It's part of the joke, you see. The ongoing irony of this place. If you don't possess a hundred per cent vision, you're thrusting your middle finger up at fate. No one is guileless enough to do that. You could tread on an alien's poisonous corpse half-buried in the mud, or fall into a toxic pit. They're everywhere, easily misconstrued for a puddle.

The landscape is open, almost desecrated. Our pre-invasion bombardment had mostly cleared its twisted almost poetically perverse vegetation. Personally, I'd rather fall into a pit. Death comes quickly. They're not deep enough to drown in, not the ones we know of anyway, but once that liquid shit gets onto you, it's over in less than an hour. Though we did hear of one poor bastard surviving an agonising nine hours. Yet, if you touch the flesh of an alien, dead or alive, the end waits patiently at the bottom of a slow, hideous spiral that goes on for weeks. Our lab cats are still promising a cure but the boys have given up on that. Promises are hollow. Maybe we should slap them with a bit of dead skin. I bet they'd work faster then.

I look to Haken, some twenty metres away. He's as jaded as I am. Behind him follows the infantry line all the way back, some thirty men and women. Anand is the only person ahead of me, a Roxi thrower in his hand. We have to be constantly alert. The aliens hide in tunnels. We discovered this the hard way. The entrances are disguised as liquid-filled pits, so we can't take a chance with any of them. Many of the pits are real, but others have false bottoms. Can you believe that? Sneaky bastards.

We halt as Anand arrives at another crater. I cover him, as does Haken. A long bluish jet of Roxi fuel squirts into the cavity, igniting the strange matter inside. It converts the pit into a phosphorous glow. It will radiate for hours. It's peculiarly alluring in the dull perpetual grey.

My eye is drawn to the right. Something sticks up through the mud. It looks like a branch. It's not. It's a leg, bent backwards. Once I identify it as human, I can easily distinguish the rest of the shape beneath the muck, like someone emerging out of a dark mist. It's a solider. Female. She's young, like the rest of us. The back of her head is missing, as though sliced off. It rests neatly on the sludge, face up. I wonder if she had time to realise that she'd been hit. Her expression is calm. I'm sure she didn't know it was coming. I hope she didn't.

None of us expect to die, or least we didn't when we first came here. We were told that there would be causalities but we didn't expect this. To be honest, I don't expect to survive. I just hope it's quick, like her. She looks like she would have been a decent person. We've lost so many. Light-filled people in their prime, taken out in the most brutal of ways. Most were with the belief that they were doing the right thing. I can't begin to tell you what it's like to listen to a buddy who you have laughed and discussed the future with (you've got to try and hang onto something, no matter how bad it gets), only to hear their screams as the septic alien cells erodes their muscles. To top it all off, the Company won't let us put them out of their misery. Their dying is the Will of God apparently, and only He can take life. I've also seen others become indifferent and turn away from the suffering of a colleague. I realise they find it difficult but I can't do that. I have to do something, even if it's just holding their hand (gloved to protect from infection). They need to feel something close to compassion, though I think I need it just as much. Sometimes they don't even know I'm there. I hang on tight, knowing it's really my humanity I'm clinging to. The others think I'm a religious flake or something, but it's the opposite. I don't tell them that because the irony is, most of them do believe, even if it's a passive conviction. When you've seen some of the things I've seen, you know that God cannot exist. To have those same believers turn their backs on their comrades, I wonder, what would your God think of you now?

I'm thankful for these Roxi pit annihilations or the Roxi Soxi, as the troops call them. Pull up your Roxi Soxi! Let's sock it to 'em, guys! It gives me time for a breather. I'm always tired. I'm never not tired. I'm never not uncomfortable. We sleep in thin, metallic cocoons, which means we can pull up camp anywhere. Those on watch have stimulants to keep awake all night. It's an eternal dusk here, gloomy but never fully dark or light. Actually, I don't mind the watch shift. The drugs take the edge off the exhaustion. It all catches up with you eventually. Then it's death on legs. I don't know how we keep going. I don't know why there aren't more mistakes. It's pure luck. That's all.

It's the little things that you miss, the ones you took for granted. We never seem to get enough to eat. The rations cover your basic requirements, but there's nothing fresh, like old-fashioned fruit and vegetables. I fantasise about fields of food. There's the true God, in that wondrous expanse of texture and diversity. I would eat any of them now, even Brussels sprouts. I could probably eat a Brussels sprouts pie. My mother would find that funny.

My body aches too. I feel old, even though I'm only twenty-three. My birthday consisted of extra rations rounded up from a few of the troops. Nice…but that was the extent of it. I just want to rest. And be warm. Curling up on a sofa would be paradise. A real shower. A decent bed. I never appreciated these things before. I was too busy worrying about a career or who my girlfriend was talking to. Though I was right to worry. She left me three weeks into my tour. So much for the 'I'll wait for you forever' spiel. Funny thing is, I didn't care that much. Forget the meaning of life. To be safe with enough food is all the meaning we'll ever need.

When I'm not daydreaming, I'm angry at them for the bullshit. They made us feel that fighting for Earth was the most distinguished, selfless act we would ever undertake. I, like a moron, believed them. Being here now, in this shit hole, I see no point in it. These creatures did nothing to us. They are human-like in some respects. They have two eyes and two legs but their face is more like an insect. They have two extra smaller arms like a marsupial. It's their actions which are interesting. I think they're curious about us. There's a possibility for communication. Well, there was…until we bombed the shit out of them. They're merely defending themselves, as is their right. It's us who are seeking out the expansion of humankind, simply because we've been stupid enough to trash our own space. We have no right being here. All we're doing is sending young people on a one-way trip to the butcher's block. It's a sick cosmic joke told by those who sit safely in their ships, distant from the carnage while they add up the numbers.

We're moving on. I haven't even registered leaving the last smouldering pit. We can go on like this for hours. Routine. But you have to remain cautious. One of us can fall at any time, struck by the enemy's silent dart, a type of thorn. We bunker down and it's a fire fight, no different than the ones that have gone on for centuries. The civilised against the savages.

This time it's going to be different. And no one sees it coming. We don't think collectively, trapped in our own private heaven (we're already living in Hell). The curse of individual thought. It will be our downfall. It is mine.

Anand arrives at another crater. He signals. We stop. He performs his check as carefully as before, no more, no less. 'Looks a little small,' he concludes.

The Roxi is not endless. It's difficult to supply in. If there's enough doubt, he'll avoid spraying. It's my job to double-check. I trust him. He's good at his job and in the nine weeks our unit's been here, he's never got it wrong. I sigh, gun in the crook of my arm. I look up at the low grey sky and yearn for the unseen stars beyond. And for the safety of the ships that hang there.

Haken says, 'If you wanna move on, we move on.'

Anand looks at his supply level. With his barrel, he traces a circle over the circumference of the pit, as though allowing the thrower to decide.

'Come on man,' says Haken, 'one way or the other. My legs are killing me.'

Anand gives one last look at the pit and then moves away.

I take a few steps to check it again. Anand didn't seem confident. It's my job to be extra vigilant. I'm professional but not everyone is. Some have begun to relish their work, taking delight in the slaughter. They can't be trusted with the responsibility of the entire unit, hence why I and others with a sturdier mindset are at the front. Still, you're pretty happy to have them around when you're burrowed in a shit-twister.

I pride myself on my ability to hold it together. I'm sure I'll make officer. If I don't die, that is. It's not that I have ambition for the corps, but it will get me out of this goddamn sewage swamp. I have to prove myself. More importantly, I have to hang on to me. Sanity is precious around here. And increasingly rare.

I feel an adrenalin rush come on like a blast of hot air. I'm right by the small crater that Anand had approved when its bottom abruptly melts away. Something emerges in a blur, so sudden I can't make it out until it's right in front of me, faster than I can react to.

Haken is behind me and can't shoot at the alien as I'm blocking his aim. He begins running in a wide arc to get a clear shot, as best he can in the mud. Anand is in a better position in front but also can't shoot as I'm behind the creature. The Roxi stream will spread out. I'm snared in the middle like a goddamn fool. We should have factored in this scenario. If I move too quickly, the creature could dash forward and claw me to death. Even if it touches me, my fate is sealed. I'd prefer the fast version. I've seen splayed corpses opened up like hacked fruit. The alien is watching me. It's also smaller than what we've seen before. A child? I didn't know they had children. I mean, I'm sure they do, I've just never seen one. Its front limbs seem underdeveloped. Its black eyes are facing forward, presumably looking at me but as the orbs are a single colour, I can't really tell. If I'm not mistaken, it's curious. It's probably never seen a human. Is it playing? Will it attack me? If I take two steps, I could touch it.

Anand is signalling but I can't hear him. I'm only aware of it. For some reason, I'm convinced it's a she. I don't know how I know this. I also sense its innocence. It hasn't reached an adolescent state yet. It doesn't want to hurt me, even though it could. It's nervous. I think it's frightened, frozen in inaction. Waiting. Like me.

I have a younger brother. When we were younger, he would look up at me, waiting for me to make a decision. I could see the trust in his face, a subtle kind of awe, just like this alien child, of which we know so little.

Haken is raising his gun. But mine is already up. I fire, an invisible, soundless pencil of atom waves. The child's body falls in on itself, its shell splintering. Its severed organs fall to the ground. I back up to prevent its fluid from splashing onto me but I don't stop firing until there is no trace of form left, only a shrivelled mass of malevolent tissue.

Harsh? My brother and I don't talk any more either. Shit goes down. That's the way things go sometimes.

Haken is looking at me.

I look back at him.

He nods. I nod.

And we move on.

All Quiet in the Bell Tower

It was one of those hot days where you can see the air rising up out of the ground. Being the holidays, people braved it nonetheless. A small fenced playground played host to three children and their supervising aunt. There was a man, not connected to them, gently gliding on a swing with his one-year-old daughter on his lap. The little girl was as thrilled as could be.

A blonde woman in her early thirties came through the gate. She was not alone. She had brought along her German shepherd. 'Ooh, let's play.'

Her boyfriend (husband?) hung back by the gate, dutiful but ill at ease.

'Come with Mummy,' she said, trying to get the dog to scale a metal latticework that led to the mouth of a slide. Was this to be her target?

A girl around eight, seeing that a large animal was on its way up, hastily went down the slide, not enjoying it the way she had planned.

With not a small amount of rear thrusting from its owner, the bewildered dog scrambled to the platform, the woman almost frothing as she joined it. 'Oooh, let's go down the sliiiiide!'

All eyes were upon her, quietly stunned, if not a touch troubled. The baby girl on the swing continued to enjoy her rush through the breeze though it was at a more languid pace than moments before, her father somewhat distracted.

The dog bobbed its head, rightfully hesitant about going down the slide at all.

'Mumsie's right behind you, sweetie! Off you go now.'

The dog, having no choice that it could discern, half scampered, half slipped down the metal embankment. It stumbled awkwardly upon hitting the ground but was unscathed as Mumsie 'Wheeeeed' down behind it.

The man with the one-year-old brought the swing to a halt, bewildered. The little girl thrust her legs, wanting more.

The woman led the dog on a fast trot around the inside perimeter of the playground, either enjoying the attention or completely unaware of it, her grin euphoric as she finally traversed the gate, where the sign clearly stated, 'No pets allowed'. The dog was seemingly thrilled to be out. Her partner trailed listlessly behind as she continued her suddenly not so merry way.

Just before they were lost from view behind a hedge, the woman was heard to say to her partner in a tone not far removed from that of a naughty pet, 'Will you hurry up? Mum and Dad are waiting!'

There was a lingering lifeless legacy at the playground, except for the baby, who had given up kicking her legs and now slumped forward, defeated.

The Long Jetty

I shuffle along the deteriorating planks of the jetty. One, two, one, two, like a rusty train. I don't remember the gaps between the planks being so large. And I certainly don't remember the jetty stretching so far out to sea. It's as though a cheeky child has pulled on it, like a piece of play dough.

I know it's based on my perception, which has changed. I really do feel it this year. Nobody wants to admit that they're old. Oops, I said it. There you go. Old, worn-out, past the use-by date, washed-up. I feel it. But I still have trouble believing it. Age. It's a pesky nuisance. Sneaks up on you. And then it's all behind you.

The ocean still smells the same, though; a mixture of its creatures and the salt, or perhaps it's the fishermen with their buckets. Dedicated. In their own world. I like that about them.

The breeze still plays the same song too. I think that's one of the things I like most about the ocean and this walk of ours, which I honour as a tradition. And yet Susan didn't like the wind. It messed up her hair. Silly woman. I used to tell her that too. Every year, the same complaint. I'd chastise her, she would tell me to shoosh and I would laugh. It was as though we would forget our routine and have to go through the whole process again the next year. Our holidays felt like an enormous record, the same speck of dust slowly coming around.

By the way, I love my record collection. I pride myself that I have never bought a CD. I believe records are back in fashion now. Stick around much longer and maybe I'll be back in fashion too.

I hear a child laughing behind me and the boards shake. I can't move in time before the kid shoots past, almost toppling me. My cane goes out. Lucky I'm quick with my hands, even if my hip is shot. I steady, redefining my centre of gravity. Little brat. The parents walk past. I watch them, waiting for an apology. They don't say a word.

People have no respect any more. In my day, the kid would have been made to say sorry. Smacked too. The shame alone would have been good enough. Good old-fashioned Catholic guilt. Did wonders for me. Not these days. We're all just a bunch of individuals bumping off each other like dodgem cars. As for us oldies, forget it. We're expendable. Toss us out with the garbage. Maybe I'll just jump off the pier here, give 'em what they want. Watch the old bastard drop.

The seagulls hang in the air. They do it for the simple point of it. I like that. It's freedom, isn't it? They shit everywhere. I better watch out in case one shits on me. There's one right in my path, as if promising to do just that. I'd like to hit it with my cane, except I'd probably dislocate my shoulder. Stupid body. It's become my enemy. I need to focus on these boards. They're a bit shabby. Could do with some maintenance. While you're there, fix me up too. The truth is, I never had a strong constitution. I wasn't one of those tough blokes. That's why it was so shocking when Susan died. Healthy as an ox. Life is rarely fair, but for want of a more palpable term, it really pissed me off. I always thought I'd go first.

Shoosh.

Susan's voice. It sounds like the wind but it isn't. She's next to me.

Shooooo…

There. I can feel her. The light pressure of her hand on my arm. The familiar fragrance of her French perfume. The comfort of her constant presence at my side. Don't look, you silly old coot. If you do, you'll know for sure that she isn't really there. Look out to sea, as you've done for over fifty years and pretend that nothing has changed.

When I reach the end of the pier, I stop to catch my breath. It's been quite a journey. We always stopped here. We would talk about this, that and the other. Before we would turn back, I'd lean forward and kiss her. She'd act all coy, like that first time, all the years before. And only yesterday. She'd look in my eyes and give me the faintest of smiles. In that brief second, before we would stroll back to the beach, I could see that she was happy. No matter what had transpired throughout the year, she was content. And loved. That moment alone was enough to keep me going for months.

I turn. But she is not there.

I listen for her voice, but the wind has taken it away.

I seek out her smell, but it is long since dispersed.

I cannot pretend. I am alone.

I should be getting used to it but at the same time, I don't want to. Yet, here on this jetty, I feel more alone than ever.

'I'm sorry, Susan,' I whisper. 'I can't come here any more.'

A nearby couple look at me. I detect the bemusement in their eyes. They think I'm talking to myself, a nutcase. The young can be so arrogant. They suddenly look away, caught out, but they're on the verge of laughing. They won't be laughing one day, when the cruelty of time takes one of them away. See how you like that.

Time…that two-faced liar. Forever wasn't nearly long enough.

I shuffle forward, but the cracks are wider and the pier seems even longer.

It's strange, after all these years, but I don't like the ocean any more.

The Elusive

I often fall for the unattainable ones. You know, the people who fall for the married types or predisposed in a fashion. For me, it's usually a girl already in a relationship, without it being cemented in a semi-irreversible commitment, like children. There has to be a sliver of hope there, like a scale glinting on a rock while the fish still twirls in the fisherman's bucket. Not exactly a romantic analogy but just as perplexing. Why does this keep happening to me?

I check out many girls as do women to men, or whatever floats your canoe. We all scan others. And if they look back, it doesn't mean anything. It's an assessment. A form of judgement. It's a flawed system but what are we supposed to do when we've only got two seconds in passing?

In a static environment, such as being seated, there's the potential for further investigation. A locking of eyes. Awkward. A look away. And then, sometimes, rarely, the repeats.

I was in trouble immediately. I was on a high bar stool by the window, leaning on a ledge support, slightly interested in the wall screen playing music videos of a generic R'n'B style, not at all interested in traffic slowly passing by and decidedly interested in her. She was seated at a small table approximately ten metres away. Close enough to detect but not enough to attract a beating. Yes, she was opposite her boyfriend. I could only see him side on. She was more direct. Perhaps seventy per cent. We linked with a gaze. A second or two. That's one look. Doesn't mean a thing. There's another. Cute. Tomboyish. Not stunning but I'm far from a desktop background.

By the third and fourth times, I began getting that feeling. A tickling sensation in my nerves, through my legs, guts, inside and out.

I look down at my beer, as though it had a whole new meaning. Maybe it did. A distraction. A saviour. I took a big gulp. Aware of everything now, especially related to self, as though trained by a stage light. I drained the glass. Put it down with purpose. Glanced across.

Damn. Unmistakable. I want her. I want her now. She wants me too. How can we make this happen? Can it really? How? She's with him. She's not uninterested in him. They're interacting in a positive way. Not a new coupling but not a faded one.

I get up. Make tracks to the bar. He can see me now. I don't dare look.

Yes. Same again please. Make small talk. Return. I take the opportunity to look again while I make myself comfortable. I drink. Sense her eyes. Sensoria. Connect. Hold. Excitement and fear pounds through my feet, up to my balls and under my ribs. Jesus, girl. Don't let him notice you.

I look away. It feels wrong. Not that I don't want it but that we could soon be caught. I'm older. A good ten years. Perhaps experience has strengthened foundations of invitation.

I look out the window. What am I doing? For fuck's sake.

This has happened to me many times. Discreet looks. Non-discreet stares. I'm going to get in trouble one day. More than before. And there's been befores… Dirty looks. Threatening looks. Confusing looks. I know what you're thinking. However, I'm not the only one at fault. It takes two to play this game. Let's face it, in youth, misunderstandings come as regular as trains on a shitty timetable.

I went to a friend's place once. Friend in a casual sense of the word. More of a work associate. We were both passionate about the film world and fancied ourselves as scriptwriters. Yet he was too brash for me. I was at that age where you accept people more readily without saying anything. Perhaps it's just me. Following a boozy post-work Friday evening, he, I and two other guys ended up at his place. His girlfriend was there. I wasn't sober but I'm pretty certain she was. She took to me like clouds to the sky. I don't know why. I'm not good-looking, not especially. Something I said? I joked around a lot. Talked shit.

Like most under the influence. Maybe it was the confidence, I don't know. She didn't try to hide her interest, however. Everyone knew. She seemed embarrassed. Almost as though she didn't want to feel that way but it was too evident to disguise.

I didn't want it either. I felt bad for her man, even though I thought he was a wanker. He wasn't aggressive. He was joking yet I could tell it troubled him. And I didn't want trouble.

She was a good-looking woman. Mid-twenties, same as me. Too awkward to manipulate around the dilemma. It caught us all by surprise. So the others and I left, leaving the couple alone, to have it out, I guess. I saw him again at work of course but not her. Never again. No happy ending. Soon after, I finished that job and I haven't seen him since. Embarrassing as it was, there's a residue of regret that lingers to the ink on this page.

The woman rises from the table and heads for the loos. We don't clock eyes but as her intent is bladder-based, I create no summation. I drink. Her man drinks. And texts, or scans the cyberwaves. What do I know? Everyone has a hundred friends, it seems.

Suddenly he seems pathetic. He's unaware of his companion's silent interaction with me. I feel sorry for him. And then I hate her. Hate what she's done to him. To me. She has all the power. I am a pawn in this charade.

Where is she? I want her back. Looking at me. I asked for this. I'm here too. I'm to blame. I don't want to get laid. I don't even want kissing. To be honest, I haven't thought beyond this discordant, broken communication. It's not about fucking. Or lust. I don't know. I think it's as simple as a hug. From someone who cares.

That's pathetic. Cuckoo. I don't know her. She could be a complete arsehole. What do I hope to achieve here? What do I want?

I look again. This time I feel something like despair. Yes. Despair. Tragedy. Melancholy. Mixed with hope. Or self-serving interest. Our primary focus. It is all about us. We are the Life. The Universe. The Love…that we deserve.

I'm doing a bad thing. I'm a shit person. Jesus, man. Drink, and shut up.

I down my beer. I need a piss. I get up. I make tracks. I design the route to go directly past their table. I give her the dirty eye as I pass, combined with the lustful eye. And the desperate eye.

I push the bathroom door aside with more force than required. I go in and piss. Which emotion did she read? Which emotion did I deliver? Do I care? Yes, I do. Too much. All the way. I could fuck her tonight. How can I get her home?

I've got to give her my number. Somehow. Set it up. Fuck her tomorrow.

Jesus. You're a fool. Forget it.

She's been looking at you.

How's it gunna happen?

You'll find a way.

Damn right I will. There's something in it. She could be something really special. This could go all the way. To the end of times. My time. There's only one chance. This one. I have to make it happen.

I wash my hands. I scrub a little water through my hair. Quick mirror check. As good as it gets.

I pull the door open with fresh confidence. Strolling through like a young Clint Eastwood. The Good, the Bad and the Horny. Let's do this!

What? Ah, fuck!

They're gone.

She's gone.

I'm gone.

Again.

www.ingramcontent.com/pod-product-compliance
Lightning Source LLC
Chambersburg PA
CBHW030211130726
47898CB00012B/983